Peck's Bad Boy at the Circus

George W. Peck

Contents

PECK'S BAD BOY AT THE CIRCUS

BY

George W. Peck

CHAPTER I.

The Bad Boy Begins a Diary--Dad Has Become Manager for a Circus--The Bad Boy Expects to Curry the Hyena and Do Stunts on the Trapeze--Ma Says Pa Will Ogle the Circassian Beauty--- Pa Buys Some Circus Clothes and Lets His Whiskers Grow.

April 10, 19..--I never thought it would come to this, that I should keep a diary, because I am not a good little boy. Nobody ever keeps a diary except a boy that wants to be an angel, and with the angels stand, or a girl that is in love, or an old maid that can't catch a man unless she writes down her emotions and leaves them around so some man will read them, and swallow the bait and not feel the hook in his gills, or a truly good bank cashier who teaches Sunday school, and skips out for Canada some Saturday night, after the bank closes, and on Monday morning they find the combination of the lock on the safe changed, and when they hire a reformed burglar to open the lock the money is all gone with the cashier. Those are the only people that ever kept a successful diary.

But I had to promise ma that I would keep a diary, so she could read it, or I never could have got her consent for me to go with pa on the road with a circus. All ma asks of me is to tell the truth about everything that happens to me and to pa during the whole summer, and I have consented, and I can see my finish, and pa's finish and ma's finish, and the finish of the circus that is going to take us along.

Gee, but we have had a hot time at our house since pa and I got back from our trip abroad. I brought pa back in better health than he was when he went away, but he has got so accustomed to excitement that I knew something would be doing pretty soon, so I was not surprised when he told us at the breakfast table that he supposed he should have to go and travel with a circus this summer.

Ma looked at pa as though she wanted to call the police and am ambulance to take him to the emergency hospital. He looked at ma and at me, speared another waffle, and said: "I know you will think I am nutty, but for almost ten years I have had a block of stock in a circus and menagerie. I went into it to help some young circus fellows, and put up quite a bunch of money, because they were honest and poor, and for a few years things went wrong, and I thought my money was gone, but for the last six years the circus has paid dividends bigger than Standard Oil, and today it stands away up among the financial successes, and the dividends on my citrus stock is better than any bank stock I have got, and it comes just like finding money. The company decided at its annual meeting to invite me to take the position of one of the managers, and I shall soon go to the winter quarters of the show, to arrange to put it on the road about the 1st of May. Now any remarks may be made, pro or con, in regard to my sanity, see?"

Well, ma swallowed something crosswise down her Sunday throat, and choked, and pa swatted her on the back so she would cough it up, and when she could speak she said: "Pa, do you have to wear tights, and jump through hoops on the back of a horse, and cut up didoes, at your time of life? For if you do I can never live to witness any such performances."

Pa was calm, and did not fly off the handle, but he just said, kindly: "Mother, you have vague ideas of the duties of the owners of a circus. The owners hire performers to do stunts, and break their necks, while we manage them and take in the shekels from the Reubens who come into town on circus day. We proprietors touch the button, and the actors and animals do the rest. I shall be a director who directs, a man who sets a dignified and pious example to the men and women who adorn the profession, coming as they do from all climes, and your pa will be the guide, philosopher and friend of all who belong to the grandest aggregation of talent ever gathered under one canvas, at one price of admission, and do not fail to witness the concert which will be given under this canvas after the main performance is over."

Ma looked at pa pretty savage, and said: "O, I see, you are going to be ringmaster, but what is to become of Hennery and me while you are cracking your whip around the hind legs of the fat woman, and ogling the Circassian beauty?"

Pa put his hand on my head and said: "Mother, Hennery will go with me, to see that I do not get into any trouble as a circus financier and general manager of the menagerie and Wild West aggregation, and hippodrome, in the great three-ring circus, and you can stay home and give us absent treatment for what ails us, and pack the money I shall send you in bales with a hay press, and put it in cold storage till we come back in the fall. It is settled, we go to conquer, and the world will lay at our feet before the middle of August, and you will be a proud woman to own a husband who will be pointed at as the most successful amusement purveyor the world has ever witnessed, and a son who will start in at the bottom round of the circus ladder and rise, step by step, until he will stand beside the great Barnum."

Ma thought seriously for a few minutes, and then she said: "O, pa, if it was anything but the circus business you and Hennery went into, like selling soap or being a bank defaulter, or something respectable, I could look the neighbors in the face, but of course if there is money in it, and you feel that the good Lord has called you to the circus field, and you will see that Hennery does not stay out nights, and Hennery will promise to see that you put on a clean collar occasionally, and you will promise me that you will not let any of those circus women in spangles make eyes at you, I will consent to your going with the circus, just this once, as the doctor has advised that you lead an active life, and I guess you will get it traveling with a circus, for it nearly killed me that time I took Hennery to see the animals, and the tent blew down, and we got separated and the sacred cow chased ma up the church steps, and Hennery and a monkey were brought home by a policeman about daylight the next morning, that time you were off fishing, and I never told you about going to the circus when you were away. So we are circus proprietors, are we? Well, it ain't so bad," and ma went upstairs to cry at our success, and pa and I went out to walk off the effects of the breaking the news to ma.

I had a long talk with pa about our changed circumstances, and asked him what I would be expected to do in the show, and he says I will fit in anywhere. He says that a boy who knows as much about everything as I think I know, but don't know a blamed thing about, will be invaluable about a show, and that going into a new business is like going to college as a freshman, as all the old circus men will haze us, and we must not expect an easy life, but one full of excitement, sleepless nights, ginger, the glare of the torchlights, the races, the flying trapeze, the smell of the sawdust and tanbark, the howling of the wild beasts, and the plaudits of the multitude of jays and jayesses, and it will be like one grand circus day spread all over the summer and fall. He says he wants me to learn the circus business from the ground up, from the currying of the hyenas with a currycomb and brush, to going up into the roof of the tent on the trapeze and falling into the net, while the audience faints with excitement. I asked pa if he wanted me to keep on playing tricks on him while we were on the road, and he said he had got so used to my tricks that he couldn't live without them, and he didn't want me to let a chance escape to make him have a good time.

April 11.--Ma and pa have had several discussions about what kind of a position it is going to leave her in, among the neighbors, for pa and I to go off with a circus, and ma wanted to withdraw from the church, and board up the windows of the house, and make folks think we had gone to the seashore, but pa convinced her that we would have preaching in the main tent every Sunday and he says there is no more pious lot of people on earth than those who travel with a circus, and then ma wanted to go along. She said she could do the mending of the long socks that the women wear when they ride barebacked, but we had to shut down on ma's going with the show, cause we never could have any fun with a woman to look after. Pa says nowadays the men and women who ride on bareback horses in the ring dress in regular evening costume, the women with low-necked dresses and long trains, and the men with swallow-tail coats and patent leather shoes, and they are as polite as dancing masters.

We have compromised with ma, and she is to meet the show at Kalamazoo and go with us to Kankakee and Keokuk until she is overcome by nervous prostration, when we shall have her go home. Pa thinks ma would last about two days with the show, but I guess if she took a course of treatment with peanuts and red lemonade one afternoon and evening, she would want to throw up her job, and go back home in charge of a stomach specialist.

Well, pa showed up at the house in his circus clothes this afternoon, and he certainly is a peach. Pa has been letting his chin whiskers grow for about six weeks, and today he had them colored black, and he looks as though he had swallowed the blacking brush, and left the bunch of bristles outside, on his chin. He looks fierce. Then, he has got a new brand of silk hat, with a wide, curling brim, and he has had a vest made of black and blue check goods, the checks as big as the checks on a checker board, and a pair of pants that look like a diamond-back rattlesnake, and he has got an imitation diamond stud in his white shirt that looks like a paper weight.

Ma wanted to know if there was any law to compel pa to dress like that, 'cause he looked as though he was a gambler or a train robber. Pa says that a circus proprietor has got to look different from anybody else, in order to inspire fear and respect on the part of the hands around the show, as well as the audiences that flock to the arena, and he asked ma if she didn't remember old Dan Rice, and old John Robinson. Ma didn't remember them, but she remembered Barnum, because Barnum lectured on temperance, and she said she hoped pa would emulate Barnum's example, and pa said he would, and then he took a watch chain with links as big as a trace chain and spread it across his checkered vest, from one pocket to the other, with a life-size gold elk hanging down the middle, and ma almost had a convulsion.

Gee, but if pa wears that rig in the menagerie tent the animals will paw and bellow like a drove of cattle that smell blood. Pa is going to wear a sack coat with his outfit, so as to look tough, and he wouldn't hear to ma when she tried to get him to wear a frock coat. He said a frock coat was all right in society or among the crowned heads, but when you have to mingle with lions and elephants one minute that would snatch the tail off a coat and chew it and the next minute you are mixed up with a bunch of freaks or a lot of bareback riders or trapeze performers, you have got to compromise on a coat that will fit any climate, and not cause invidious remarks, whatever that is.

I will have to stand up beside the giant once in a while to show the difference in the size of men, and at other times I will have to stand beside the midgets and look like a giant myself. We are all packed up, and in two days we start for the winter quarters of the show, to pound it into shape for the road. By ginger, I can't hardly wait to get there and see pa boss things.

CHAPTER II.

The Bad Boy Visits the Circus in Winter Quarters--He Meets the
Circus Performers--Dad Rides a Horse and Gets Tossed in a
Blanket--The Bad Boy Goes "Kangarooing"--Pa's Clothes Cause
Excitement Among the Animals--A Monkey Steals His Watch.

April 15.--We are now at the winter quarters of the show, in a little town,
on a farm just outside, where the tent is put up and the animals are being cared for in barns, and the performers are limbering up their joints,
wearing overcoats to turn flip-flaps, and everybody has a cold, and looks
blue, and all are anxious for warm weather.

Pa created a sensation when we arrived by his stunning clothes, his jet black
chin whiskers and his watch chain over his checkered vest, and when the proprietors introduced pa to the performers and hands, as an old stockholder in the show,
who would act as assistant manager during the season and pa smiled on them with
a frown on his forehead, and said he hoped his relations with them would be pleasant, one of the old canvasmen remarked to a girl who rides two horses at once with
the horses strapped together, so they can't get too far apart and cause her to break
in two, said that old goat with the silk hat would last just about four weeks, and
that he reminded the canvasman of a big dog which barked at people as though he
would eat them, and at the same time wagged his tail, so people would not think he
was so confounded dangerous.

The principal proprietor of the circus told pa to make himself at home around
the tent, and not be offended at any pleasantry on the part of the attaches of the
show, for they were full of fun, and he went off to attend to some business and left
pa with the gang. They were practicing riding bare-backed horses around the ring,
with a rope hitched in a belt around the waist of the rider and an arm swinging

around from the center pole, so if they fell off the horse the rope would prevent the rider from falling to the ground, a practice that the best riders adopt early in the season, the same as new beginners, 'cause they are all stiffened up by being out of practice. One man rode around a few times, and pa got up close to the ring and was making some comments such as: "Why, any condemned fool could ride a horse that way," when the circus gang as quick as you could say scat, fastened a belt around pa's stomach, that had a ring in it, and before he knew it they had hitched a snap in the ring, and pa was hauled up as high as the horse, and his feet rested on the horse's back, and the horse started on a gallop.

Well, say, pa was never so surprised in his life, but he dug his heels into the horse's back, and tried to look pleasant, and the horse went half way around the ring, and just as pa was getting confidence some one hit the horse on the ham with a piece of board, and the horse went out from under pa and he began to fall over backwards, and I thought his circus career would end right there, when the man who had hold of the rope pulled up, and pa was suspended in the air by the ring in the belt, back up, and stomach hanging down like a pillow, his watch dangling about a foot down towards the ring, and the horse came around the ring again and as he went under pa, pa tried to get his feet on the horse's back, but he couldn't make it work, and pa said, as cross as could be: "Lookahere, you fellers, you let me down, or I will discharge every mother's son of you."

But they didn't seem to be scared, for one man caught the horse and let it out of the ring, and the man who handled the rope tied it to the center pole by a half hitch, and the fellows all went into the dressing room to play cinch on the trunks, leaving pa hanging there. Just then the boss canvasman came along and he said: "Hello, old man, what you doing up there?" And pa said some of the pirates in the show had kidnaped him, and seemed to be holding him up for a ransom, and he said he would give ten dollars if some one would let him down.

The boss canvasman said he could fix it for ten, all right, and he blew a whistle, and the gang came back, and the boss said: "Bring a blanket and help this gentleman down;" so they brought a big piece of canvas, with handles all around it, and about a dozen fellows held it, and the rope man let pa down on the canvas, and unhitched the ring, and when pa was in the canvas he laughed and said: "Thanks, gentlemen, I guess I am mot much of a horseback rider," and then the fellows pulled on the handles of the canvas, and by gosh, pa shot up into the air half-way to the top of the tent, and when he came down they caught him in the canvas and tossed him up a whole lot of times until pa said: "O, let up, and make it $20." Just then the proprietor who had introduced pa to the men came in and saw what was going on, and he said: "Here, you heathen, you quit this hazing right here," and they let pa down on the floor of the ring, and he got up and pulled his pants down, that had got up above his knees, and shook himself and took out his roll, and peeled off a $20 bill and gave it to the canvasman, and he shook hands with them all, and said he liked a joke as well as anybody, and for them to spend the money to have a good time, and they all laughed and patted pa on the back, and said he was a dead game sport, and would be an honor to the profession, and that now that he has taken the first degree as a circus man he could call on them for any sacrifice, or any work, and he would find that they would be Johnny on the spot.

Then he went out to the dining tent and took dinner with the crowd and had a jolly time. There was a woman trapeze performer on one side of pa at dinner, and she began to kick at once about the meals, and when the waiter brought a piece of meat to us all--a great big piece, that looked like corned beef, she said: "For heaven's sake, ain't that elephant that died all been eaten up yet?" and then she told pa that they had been fed on that deceased elephant, until they all felt like they had trunks growing out of their heads, and pa poked the meat with his fork, and thought it was elephant, and he lost his appetite, and everybody laughed. I eat some of it and if it was elephant it was all right.

Well, when dinner was about over, all filled their glasses to drink to the health of pa, the old stockholder and new manager, and pa got up and bowed, and made a little speech, and when he sat down one of the circus girls was in his chair, and he sat in her lap, and the crowd all yelled, except a Spanish bull-fighter who seemed to be the husband of the woman pa sat on, and he wanted pa's blood, but the old circus manager took him away to save pa from trouble, and he glared back at pa, and I think he will stab pa with a dirk knife.

We got out of the dining tent, and went to the barn, where the animals are kept all winter, and pa wanted me to become familiar with the habits of the beasts, 'cause they were to be in pa's charge, with the keepers of the different kinds of animals to report to pa. Nobody need tell me that animals have no human instincts, and do not know how to take a joke. We are apt to think that wild animals in captivity are worrying over being confined in cages, and gazed at and commented on by curious visitors, and that they dream of the free life they lived in the jungles, and sigh to go back where they were, captured, and prowl around for food, but you can't fool me. Animals that formerly had to go around in the woods, hungry half the time and occasionally gorging themselves on a dead animal and sleeping out in the rain in all kinds of weather, know when they have struck a good thing in a menagerie, with clean straw to sleep in, and when they are hungry all they have to do is to sound their bugle and they have pre-digested beefsteak and breakfast food brought to them on a silver platter, and if the food is not to their liking they set up a kick like a star boarder at a boarding house. Their condition in the show, in its changed condition from that of their native haunts, is like taking a hobo off the trucks of a freight train and taking him to the dining car of the limited, and letting him eat to a finish. People talk about animals escaping from captivity, and going back to the jungles and humane societies shed tears over the poor, sad-eyed captives, sighing for their homes, but you turn them loose at South Bend, and run your circus train to New Albany without them and they would follow the train and overtake it before the evening performance the next day, and you would find them trying to break into their cages again, and they would have to be fed.

When pa and I went into the barn where the cages were, to take an account of stock, and get acquainted with our animals, they acted just like the circus men did when they saw pa's clothes. The animals were about half asleep when we went in, but a big lion bent one eye on pa, and then he rose up and shook himself and gave a roar and a cough that sounded like he had the worst case of pneumonia, and he snorted a couple of times, as though he was saying to the other animals: "Here's something that will kill you dead, and I want you all to have a piece of it, raw," and he brayed some more, and all the animals joined in the chorus, the big tiger lying down on his stomach and waving his tail, and snarling and showing his teeth like a cat that has located a mouse hole, and the tiger seemed to say: "O, I saw it first, and it's mine."

The hyena set up a laugh like a man who is not tickled, but feels that it is up to him to laugh at a funny story that he can't see the point of at a banquet where Chauncey Depew tells one of his crippled jokes, and pa was getting nervous. A big grizzly bear was walking delegate in his cage, and he looked at pa as much as to say: "Hello, Teddy, I was not at home when you called in Colorado, but you get in this cage, and I will make you think the Spanish war was a Sunday school picnic beside what you will get from your uncle Ephraim," and a bob cat jumped up into the top of his cage and snarled and showed his teeth, and seemed to say: "Bring on your whole pack of dogs and I will eat them alive."

Pa threw out his chest in front of a monkey cage, and a monkey snatched his watch, and then all the animals began to laugh at pa just like a lot of bad boys in school when visitors make a call. Pa went around to visit all the animals, officially, while I got interested in a female kangaroo, with a couple of babies, not more than three weeks old, and I noticed the mother kangaroo made the old man kangaroo, her husband, stand around and he acted just like some men I have seen who were afraid to say their souls were their own in the presence of their wives.

The female kangaroo is surely a wonder, and seems to be built on plans and specifications different from any other animal, cause she has got a fur-lined pouch on her stomach, just like a vest, that she carries her young in. When the babies are frightened they make a hurry-up move towards ma, the pouch opens, and they jump in out of sight, like a gopher going into its hole, and the mother looks around as innocent as can be, as much as to say: "You can search me. I don't know, honestly, where those kids have gone, but they were around here not more than a minute ago." And when the fright is over the two heads peep out of the top of the pouch, and the old man grunts, as much as to say: "O, come on out, there is no danger, and let your ma have a little rest, 'cause she is nervous," and then the babies come out and run around the cage, and sit up on their hind feet and look wise. That kangaroo pouch is a success, and I wonder why nature did not provide pouches for all animals to carry their young in. I think Pullman must have got his ideas for the upper and lower berths of a sleeping car by seeing a kangaroo pouch. I am going to study the kangaroo and make friends with the old man kangaroo, 'cause he looks as though he had troubles of his own.

Pa showed up without any coat, while I was kangarooing, and there was a rip in his pants, and I asked him what was the trouble, and he said he got too near the cage of a leopard that seemed to be asleep, and the traitor reached out his paw and gathered in the tail of pa's coat, and just snatched it off his back as though it was made of paper.

Pa is a little discouraged about his experience in the circus the first day, but he says it will be great when we get the run of the business. He says every day will have its excitement. Tomorrow they are going to extract a tooth from the boa-constrictor, and pa and I are going to help hold him, while the animal dentist pulls the tooth, and then we scrub the rhinoceros, and oil the hippopotamus, and get everything ready to start out on the road, and I can't write any more in my diary until after we fix the snake. Gee, but he is as long as a clothesline.

CHAPTER III.

Pa Reproves the Fat Woman for Losing Flesh--The Bearded Lady Faints in Pa's Arms--The Bad Boy Introduced Into Animal Society--They Pull the Boa Constrictor's Ulcerated Tooth.

Winter Quarters of the Only Circus, April 20.--Pa has had a hard job today. The boss complained to pa that the fat woman had been taking anti-fat, or dieting, or something, 'cause she was losing flesh, and the living skeleton was beginning to fat up. He wanted pa to call them into the office and have a diplomatic talk with them about their condition, 'cause if this thing continued they would ruin the show.

So pa went to the office and sent for them, and I was there as a witness, in case of trouble. The fat woman came in first, and there was no chair big enough for her, so she sat down on a leather lounge, which broke and let her down on the floor, and pa tried to help her up, but it was like lifting a load of hay. So he leaned her against the wall and said:

"Madame, the management has detailed me to censure you for losing flesh, and I am instructed to say if you do not manage to take on about fifty pounds more flesh before the show starts on the road, you don't go along. What you want to do is to eat more starchy food and sleep more at night. They tell me you go out nights to dances and drink high balls, and this has got to stop. Drink beer and eat cheese sandwiches at night, or it is all off. This show can't afford to take along no 400-pound fairy for a fat woman when the contract calls for a 500-pound mountain of flesh, see?" and pa looked just as stern as could be.

The fat woman began to cry and sob, so it sounded like an engine blowing off steam, and she told pa that the cause of her losing flesh was that she was in love with the living skeleton, and that he had been paying attention to the bearded woman, and she would scratch her eyes out if she could catch her. Just then the living skeleton came in, and when he saw the fat woman sitting on the floor crying, and pa talking soothing to her and telling her he could appreciate her condition, 'cause he had been in love some hisself, the skeleton pushed pa away and tried to lift it, and said: "What is the matter with my itty tootsy-wootsy, and what has the bad old man with spinach on his chin been doing to you?"

Then he turned on pa and his legs began to shake and rattle like a pair of bones in a minstrel show, and he said: "I will hold you responsible for this." Pa said he was not going to interfere in the love affairs of any of the freaks, and just then the bearded woman came in, and when she saw the living skeleton holding the hand of the fat woman, who sat on the floor like a balloon blowed up, the bearded woman gave a kick at the living skeleton which sounded like clothes bars falling down in the laundry, and she grabbed the fat woman's blonde wig and pulled it off, and then the bearded woman began to cry and she threw herself into pa's arms and began to sob on his bosom and mingle her whiskers with his.

Pa yelled for help, and I thought it was time for me to be doing something, so I went outside the office to the fire alarm box and touched a button, and then I run like thunder for the police, and the firemen came with the extinguishers and began to throw chemically charged water into the room, and the police dragged out the fat woman, who had fainted, and the living skeleton, whom she had pulled down into her lap, and laid them out in the ring, and then they got hold of pa and pulled him out, and the bearded woman had fainted in pa's arms and the stove was tipped over and was setting fire to the furniture and they brought the bearded woman and the fat woman to their senses by pouring water on them from a hose. Finally they were sent to their quarters, and the other owner of the show came to pa and said he hoped this would be the last of that kind of business, as long as pa remained with the show, that one of the rules was that no man in an executive capacity must under any circumstances take any liberties with any of the females connected with the show.

Pa was hot, and said when women got crazy in love no man was safe, and the other owner of the show said that was all right this time, but not to let it occur again, and pa tried to explain how the bearded woman came to jump on to him and faint in his arms, but the owner said: "That is all right, but you can't hold 'em in your arms before folks," and then pa offered to whip any man who said he was in love with any bearded woman, and he pulled off his coat. Just then I came along and told the whole story, and then the crowd all had a good laugh, and pa took them all out and treated.

I guess it is all settled now, 'cause the living skeleton and the fat woman have got permission to get married, the bearded lady is sweet on pa, and a girl has just joined the show, who walks a wire, and she says I am about the sweetest thing that ever came down the pike, and I guess this show business is all right, all right.

April 21.--We are getting acquainted with the animals, and it is just like going into society.

There is the aristocracy, which consists of the high born animals, the middle class and the low down, common herd, and when you go among the animals as strangers you are received just as you would be in society. If you are properly intro-duced to the elephants by the elephant keeper, who vouches for your standing and honor, the elephants take to you all right and extend to you certain courtesies, same as society people would invite you to dinner, but if you wander around and sort of butt in, the elephants are on to you in a minute and roll their eyes at you and look upon you as a common "person," and if you attempt any familiarity they look at you as much as to say: "Sir, I am not allowed to associate with any except the 400." Then they turn their backs and act so much like shoddy aristocracy that you would swear they were human.

I remember when pa was first in the elephant corral, the keeper forgot to tell the big elephant who pa was, and when the keeper raised up one foot of the el-ephant and examined a corn, pa went up and pinched a bunch on the elephant's leg and said to the keeper: "That looks to me like a spavin," and he nebbed it hard. Well, the elephant groaned like a boy with a stone bruise on his heel, and before pa knew what was coming the elephant wound his trunk under pa and raised pa upon his tusks and was going to toss him in the air and catch him as he came down and walk on him, when pa yelled murder and the keeper took an iron hook and hooked it into the elephant's skin, and said: "Let that man down," and he let pa down easy, and the keeper some way showed the elephant that pa was one of the owners of the show, and that elephant acted just as human as could be, for he fairly toadied to pa, like a society leader that has given the cold shoulder to some one that is as good or better than they, or like an impudent employee who has insulted his employer and is afraid of losing his job. After that whenever pa and I go around the elephants they bow down to us, and I think I could take an iron hook and drive an elephant anywhere.

There are all classes among the animals in a menagerie the same as human society. The lions are like the leaders of society who are well born and proud but poor. They are always invited everywhere, but never entertain, though they kick and find fault and ogle everybody and look wise and distinguished.

The sacred cattle are too good to live and pose as the pious animals who do not want to associate with the bad animals and are constantly wearing an air of "I am holier than any of you," but they will reach through the bars of their cage and steal alfalfa from the Yak and the mule deer, and if they kick about it the sacred cattle look hurt and act like it was part of their duty to take up a collection, and they bellow a sort of hymn to drown the kicking.

The different kind of goats in a menagerie are the butters-in, or the new rich, who get in the way of the society leaders and try to outdo them in society stunts, but they smell so that the other animals are made sick and the goats are only tolerated because animal society is afraid to offend them, for fear the leaders may some time go into bankruptcy and the goats will take their places and never let them get a smell of the good things of life.

The bears are the working people of the show, and the big grizzlies are the walking delegates who control the amalgamated association of working bears, and the occupants of the other cages have got to cater to Uncle Ephraim, the walking delegate, or be placed on the unfair list and slugged.

The hyenas and the jackals and the wolves represent the anarchists who are down on everybody in the show, who won't do a thing to help along and won't allow any other animal to do anything, and who seem to want to burn and slay, to carry a torch by night and poison by day, and want everything in the show to be chaos. Those animals are never so happy as when the wind and lightning strike the tent, and blow it down and kill people and create a panic, and then these anarchists sing and laugh and enjoy their peculiar kind of animal religion.

The zebras and giraffes are the dudes of the show, and you can imagine, if they were human, they would play tennis and golf, drive four in hands and pose to be admired, while the Royal Bengal tigers, if they were half human, would drive automobiles at the rate of a mile a minute on crowded streets, run over people and never stop to help the wounded, but skip away with a sneer, as much as to say: "What are you going to do about it?"

The hippopotamus is like the lazy fat man that groans from force of habit, sits down as though it was the last act of his life and only gets up when the bell rings for meals, and he sweats blood for fear he will lose his meal ticket and starve to death.

The seals are the clean-cut Baptists of the show, who believe in immersion, and they have more brain than any animals in the show, because they live on a fish diet, though they have a pneumonia cough that makes you feel like sending for a doctor.

Gee, but last night when we thought spring had come and we could start on the road pretty soon, the snow fell about a foot deep, and it was so cold that all the animals howled all night, and shivered, and went on a regular strike. We had to put blankets on them, and no one of them seemed to be comfortable except the polar bears, the arctic foxes and the fat woman. The other owners of the show thought it was a good time to take the boa constrictor and pull an ulcerated tooth, 'cause he was sort of dumpish, so pa and I helped hold the snake, which is about twenty feet long.

Pa was up near the snake's head, and when the man with the forceps got hold of the tooth and gave it a yank, the confounded snake come to and began to stand on his head and thrash around, and pa dropped his hold and started to climb the center pole, but he got caught in a gasoline torch, and they had to turn a hose on pa, and he was awful scared, 'cause he always did hate snakes, but they gave the snake chloroform and got him quiet, and pa came down, and they gave him a pair of baggy trousers belonging to the clown, to go to dinner in, and pa was a sight.

CHAPTER IV.

Pa Finds the Fat Lady a Burden--The Bad Boy Makes His First Public Appearance--He Talks Politics with the Midget--Pa Meets with Numerous Accidents.

May 1.--We had the darndest time getting packed up and started on the road. How in the name of heaven we ever got half the things on the cars is more than I know, but it seems as though the circus company had a man to look after everything, and he had men under him to look after his regular share of things, so when the cars were loaded, and the boss clapped his hands, and the engineer tooted his whistle, there wasn't a tent stake or a rope, or a board seat, or anything left behind. Every man knew exactly where the things were that he was responsible for, so he could lay his hands on them in the dark, and he knew just what wagon his stuff was to go in.

Gee, but you talk about system, there is no business in the world that has a system like a show on the road. Every performer was in his or her section in the sleeper, and pa and I got an end section with the freaks, the fat woman across the aisle from us. That fat woman is going to make life a burden for pa, I can see that plain enough. She is engaged to the living skeleton, and he sleeps in the upper berth, over her, and he is jealous of pa, while the fat woman has got to depending on pa to do little things for her.

Of course, the first night out is always the worst on a sleeper, and the poor woman is nervous, and when the animal train, in the second section, ran on a side track beside our train of sleepers, and Rajah, the boss lion, got woke up and exploded one of his roars, within six feet of the fat woman's berth, she just gave one yell, and reared up, and came down hard in the berth. Something broke, and she went right through the bottom of the berth to the floor, doubled up like a jackknife.

Pa got up and went to her berth, though I told him to keep away, 'cause he would get into trouble. First he stumbled over one of her shoes, and said he thought he had told everybody to keep their telescope valises in the baggage car, and that made her mad. Then he reached in the berth and got hold of one of her feet, and pa got the men to help and they got her out, but she seemed all squshed together. She sat up all night and wanted to lean on pa, but the skeleton kept his head over the rail of the upper berth and his snake-like eye never left pa all night.

The bearded woman got up out of her berth about daylight, to go to the toilet room for a shave, or a hair cut, or something, and when she saw pa trying to soothe the fat woman and hold her from breaking in two, she screamed and slapped pa's face, and had a mess of hysterics. The fat woman grabbed a couple of handfuls of female whiskers, and was going to pull them out by the roots, when the bearded woman begged her not to pull them out, as to lose her whiskers would destroy her means of livelihood.

Then the bugle blew for everybody to get up and go to the show lot, and put up the tents for the first show of the season. When we got out of the sleeper we asked where we were, and a man told pa we were at Peoria, Ill., and he wanted pa to give him a complimentary ticket for telling what town we were in, but pa looked fierce at the man and asked what kind of an easy mark he took him for, and the man slunk away. You wouldn't think they could unload those two trains of cars, about 80 in all, in a week, but when we got out the horses were hitched on the wagons, and in 15 minutes they were loaded and on the way to the lot, and pa and I got on the first wagon.

Talk about system. The surveyors were there ahead of us, and had measured off the lot and pushed wire stakes in the ground where the grub tent was to be, and when the first wagon of the grub outfit arrived, which contained a big range, big enough to cook for a thousand men, stove pipes were put on, which telescoped up into the air, and in two minutes a fire was built and bacon and potatoes and coffee were cooking, local bread wagons were unloading bread on the grass, 50 men put up poles and spread the tent on, and others set up tables in the tent, and in half an hour breakfast was served to the first 500 men. Pa and I drew up to the first table, but there was a yell to "put 'em out," and we found we had sat down to the table of the negro canvasmen, and they struck because they would not associate on an equality with white trash.

Gee, but pa was mad. He said he was as good as any nigger, and that made them mad and they threw boiled potatoes and scrambled eggs at pa, and we had to retire, but when pa complained to the boss canvasman, he told pa to go and eat with the freaks and try and keep in his place.

We got breakfast at another table, and then we went out on the lot to superintend the putting up of the big tents. The greatest thing was a wagon containing a miniature pile driver, run by steam, which was driven around outside of where the big tents were to be, and it drove down the big stakes so quick it would make your head swim, and the grounds were covered with Peoria people who wanted to see how it was done.

Pa imitated the boss canvasman by walking around the lot with his coat over his arm, and a dirty shirt on, trying to look tough, and he bossed the sightseers about, and acted cross, and told a man and woman with a baby wagon to get off the lot, but pa was called down by the principal owner of the show good and plenty.

Said the owner to pa: "Remember, the success of our show depends on the friendship and good will of the people who think enough of us to come out to see us set up keeping house, and that they are all our guests, and if they get in our way we should go around them, and look pleasant. We must not get the big head and show that our hair pulls, and that we are tired and cross. This is a place of amusement, and all connected with the show are expected to heal up sores, instead of causing bruises, and if you ever see an employee of this show treating a visitor unkindly, send him to the ticket wagon to get his wages, and tell him to go away quick, and stay away long."

You could have lit a match to pa's face, it was so red hot, but he learned a lesson, for I saw him holding a tired mother's baby up on his shoulders, so it could see the drove of camels come up to the lot from the train, soon after. It was great to see all the tents go up as if raised by machinery, and after all were erected, and the rings were graded, and the animals in the menagerie tent all fed and watered, and the performers in the dressing-room ready for the afternoon performance, pa was the proudest man ever was. He walked all around, inspecting everything, and kicking occasionally at something that got balled up, and when the crowd came to buy tickets, he stood around the grand entrance, looking wise, and he was so good natured that he bet ten dollars he could guess which walnut shell a bean was under, which a three-card monte man was losing money at, and pa lost his ten with a smile. He said he wanted to be kind to the patrons of the show.

This was my first appearance in the show business. I had to stand up beside the giant, to show how little I was, and then I had to stand up beside the midget to show how big I was compared with him. It went all right with the giant, because he was so big I was afraid of him, but I thought the midget was about my age, and needed protection, and when the crowd surged around us I said: "Don't be afraid, little fellow, I will see that no one harms you." The look he gave me was enough to freeze water.

When the crowd had gone into the big show tent, what do you think, that confounded midget began to ask me how I stood on the tariff question, and he argued for free trade, whatever that is, for half an hour, and made me think of Bryan during a campaign, and then he branched off on to the Monroe doctrine, which I suppose is something connected with a rival show, and I guess he would be talking yet, only a big husky fellow came along, a fellow about 25 years old, and he stooped over and put his hand on the midget's shoulder and said: "Hello, dad," and by gosh, the midget introduced me to the big galoot as his youngest son. Wouldn't that skin you.

The first day of the season was great, only all the performers had not got limbered up. One of the girls on the flying trapeze fell off into the net from the roof of the tent and broke her suspenders, so when they got her down in the ring it seemed as though everything she had on was going to shuck loose, and leave her with nothing but a string of beads, and pa went up to wrap his coat around her, and she kicked his hat off and ran into the dressing-room. The audience just yelled, and pa blushed scarlet, 'cause he saw it was a put-up job to make him ridiculous.

During the chariot races pa had to jump like a box car to keep from being run over by a four-horse chariot driven by a one-horse girl, and the attendants dragged pa out from under a bunch of horses being ridden barebacked, like fury. Then two horses hitched together with a strap were being ridden by a woman, the strap broke and the horses spread apart, and some one yelled that she had split clear in two. Pa rushed in to help carry one half of her into the dressing-room, but she wasn't hurt at all, 'cause the peanut boy told me she was a rubber woman, and you could stretch her half way across the ring, and she would come together all right, and eat a hearty meal. Gee, but a circus is a great place to study human nature.

In the evening performance at Peoria there came up a windstorm which blew down part of the menagerie tent, where the freaks were, and when the storm was over, and the tent top was pulled up again, they found pa all right. He started to crawl under the canvas, and skip out for fear of the animals, but the fat lady caught him and sat down on him.

WITH THE CIRCUS

CHAPTER V.

The Rogue Elephant Creates a Panic and Pa Proves Himself a Hero--The Bad Boy Gets Scolded for "Being Tough"--He Finds That Audiences Like Accidents.

May 6.--We had the worst time at Akron last week and pa proved himself a hero, though he was swatted good by the rogue elephant before he got his second wind and went for the animal.

We have a male elephant that is almost human, 'cause he gets on a tear about once a month, like a regular ugly husband. You can't tell when his mind is in condition for running amuck, but suddenly he will whoop like a drunken man, strike his poor patient wife over the back with his trunk and grab her tail and try to pull it out by the roots, and jump up and crack his heels together like a drunken shoemaker, and bellow as though he was saying he was a bad man from Bitter Creek.

Well, at Akron, the keeper of this elephant, Bolivar, had to go and see a girl that he met when the show was here last year, and settle a case of breach of promise before a justice of the peace, and the boss told pa to look after the elephant for an hour or so. So pa took a pole with a hook in it and sat down on a bale of hay to watch Bolivar. It was one of those hot days, and Bolivar stood drooping and perspiring, and wishing the show was in Alaska, and pa was kind of sleepy, like everybody in the show, when suddenly that elephant whooped, and swatted Jeanette, his wife, a couple of times, and she cried pitiful, and pa put the hook in Bolivar's hide and gave a jerk, and told him to hush up that noise, but Bolivar just reared and pitched and walked right through the side of the menagerie tent, and seemed to say to the other animals: "Come on, boys; there is going to be something doing," and the animals all set up a howl in their own language, as though they were saying: "Whooper up, old man, and don't let them monkey with you."

Bolivar went out in the street and mowed a wide swath, with pa after him, hooking him all the time, but he paid no attention to pa. He put his head under the side of a street ear loaded with negroes that had come to see the show, dressed in their Sunday clothes, and tipped the car over on the side, and the negroes crawled through the windows and went uptown yelling murder, while Bolivar went in front of a grocery store where there was a pile of watermelons, and began to throw them at the people in the street, and the negroes thought an elephant was not so bad, so they came back and had a feast.

Pa tried to head off Bolivar at the grocery, but Bolivar took half a watermelon and put the red side on top of pa's head, and squashed it down so the seeds and juice and pulp ran down pa's shirt and neck, and he looked as though murder had been committed, but pa wiped his face on his shirt sleeve and showed game, because he kept mauling Bolivar with the hook. Bolivar broke up a millinery store by throwing tomatoes at the women in the windows, and he went into a yard where a woman was washing and squirted the bluing water all over the woman, and all over pa, and then he chewed the clothes on the line, and drove the family over the fence.

You'd a died to see those milliners climb over a high board fence head first, and Bolivar actually seemed to laugh. Bolivar run one of his tusks through a barrel of gasoline, and it run out on the street car track, and an electric spark set it on fire, and the fire department turned out, but the engines had to all go around Bolivar, 'cause he wouldn't budge an inch, but seemed to say: "Let 'er rip, boys; this is the Fourth of July."

The circus men began to come with ropes and clubs, to tie Bolivar and throw him, but he escaped into a side street and watched the engines put out the fire, and he swung around with his trunk and tusks and wouldn't let anyone come near him but pa with the hook, and he seemed to enjoy the prodding, but I guess that gave him courage to keep on doing things.

The principal proprietor of the show came along, and when he saw pa with watermelon and bluing water all over him, and perspiration rolling down his face, he said to pa: "Why don't you take your elephant back to the lot, 'cause the afternoon performance is about to begin," and that made pa mad, and he said: "You go on with your afternoon performance, and I will have Bolivar there all right," and then everybody laughed, but pa knew what he was about.

Pa dropped his hook and went to a hose cart and took a Babcock extinguisher and strapped it on his back and went up to Bolivar, who was tipping over some dummies in front of a clothing store, and pa said: "Bolivar, you lay down," but Bolivar threw a seven-dollar suit of clothes at pa, and bellowed, as much as to defy pa. Pa turned the cock of the extinguisher, and pointed the nozzle at Bolivar's head, and began to squirt the medicated water all over him. For a moment Bolivar acted as though he couldn't take a joke, and was going to start off again, but pa kept squirting, and when the chemical water began to eat into Bolivar's hide, the big animal weakened, and trumpeted in token of surrender, and kneeled down in front of pa, and finally got down so pa could get on his back, and pa took the hook and hooked it in the flap of Bolivar's ear, where is a tender spot, and he told Bolivar to get up and go back to the tent, and Bolivar was as meek as a lamb, and he got up, with pa on his back, and the fire extinguisher on pa's back, and marched back to the tent, through the hole he had made coming out. Thousands of people followed, and cheered pa, and when they got in the tent pa said to the principal owner of the show, who had made fun of him: "Here's your elephant, and whenever any of your old animals get on the warpath, and you want 'em rounded up, don't forget my number, 'cause I can knock the spots out of any animal except a giraffe." The crowd cheered pa again and he got down off the elephant, took off his fire extinguisher, and handed Bolivar a piece of rag carpet, and said: "Eat it, you old catamaran, or I'll kill you," and Bolivar was so scared of pa he eat the carpet, which shows the power of brain over avoirdupois, pa says.

The regular keeper of Bolivar heard he was on the rampage, and he came back on the run to conquer him, after pa had got him back in the tent, but Bolivar looked at him with a faraway look in his eyes, as much as to say: "Seems to me I have met you somewhere before, but a new king has been crowned," and he took his old keeper by the back of his coat and threw him toward the monkey cage. The monkeys gave the keeper the laugh, and Bolivar put his trunk lovingly on pa's shoulder, and seemed to say: "Old man, you are it, from this time out." Pa looked proud, and the old keeper looked sick. The people in the show are going to present pa with a loving cup, and I guess he can run the menagerie part of the show.

When the freaks heard of pa's bravery, the fat woman and the bearded lady wanted to hug pa, but pa waved them away, and said he liked the elephant business best.

May 7.--I used to think that if I could belong to a circus, and go away with it when it left the town I lived in, that it would be pretty near going to heaven. I used to hope for the time when I would get nerve enough to run away, and go with a circus, and wear a dirty shirt, and be around a tent and wash off the legs of a spotted horse with castile soap, and when people gathered about me to watch the proceedings, to look tough and tell them in a hoarse voice way down my throat, sort of husky from sleeping in the wet straw with the spotted horse, that they must go on about their business, and not disturb the horse.

I had thought if I should run away and go with a circus, some day, when I got far enough away from ma, that I would up and swear, and be tough, and when I came home in the fall, and the neighbor boys would come around me, I would chew tobacco and tell them of the joys of circus life. Well, maybe I will some day, but at present I am sleepy all the time.

We have showed six times the last week, and traveled a thousand miles, and it seems as though there is nothing doing but putting up and taking down tents, and going to and from the cars, and you can't be tough, 'cause there is always some boss around to tell you to look pleasant if you are cross, and to tell you to change your shirt or get out of the show, and if you swear at anything you are called down.

Pa and I put in a good deal of time during the afternoon and evening performances in the dressing-room, near the door leading to the main tent. That is the nearest to being in an insane asylum of any place I was ever in. The performers get ready for their several acts in bunches or families, all in one spot, and they act serious and jaw each other, and each bunch acts as though their act was all there was to the show, and if it was cut out for any reason, the show would have to lay up for the season, when in fact each one is only a cog in the great wheel, and if one cog should slip, the wheel would turn just the same. These people never smile before they go in the ring, but just act as though too much depended on them to crack a smile. When a bunch is called to go in the ring, they all look at each other as though it was the parting of the ways, and they clasp hands and go out of the dressing-room as though walking on eggs. When they get in the ring they look around to see if all eyes are upon them, and bow to people who are looking at something going on in another ring, and who don't see them, and then they go through their performance with everybody looking somewhere else.

When the act is over the audience seems glad, and clap their hands because they are polite, and it don't cost anything to clap hands, and the performers turn some more flip flaps, and go running out to the dressing-room, and take a peek back into the big tent as though expecting an encore, but the audience has forgotten them and is looking for the next mess of performers, and the ones who have just been in go and lie down on straw and wonder if they can hit the treasurer for an advance on their salaries, so they can go to a beer garden and forget it all.

An average audience never gets its money's worth unless some one is hurt doing some daring act. Pa suggested that they have some one pretend to be hurt in every act, and have them picked up and carried out on stretchers with doctors wearing red crosses on their arms in attendance, giving medicine and restoratives. The show tried it at Bucyrus, O., and had seven men and two women injured so they had to be carried out, and the audience went wild, and almost mobbed the dressing-room, to see the doctor operate on the injured. It was such a great success that next week we are going to put in an automobile ambulance and have an operating table in the dressing-room with a gauze screen so the audiences can see us cut off legs like they do in a hospital. Maybe we shall put in a dissecting room if the people seem to demand it.

CHAPTER VI.

The Bad Boy Puts Fly-Paper in the Bob Cat's Cage--The Bob Cat Causes a Panic in the Main Tent--The Midget Quarrels with the Giant--Pa is Almost Arrested for Kidnaping and the Ostrich Swallows His Diamond Stud.

May 14.--This has been a week that would kill anybody, and pa and I talk of resigning, though pa feels as though he didn't want to break up the show by going away right in the middle of the harvesting of shekels from the country men, and I don't know what would happen if pa and I should both be taken sick at the same time.

The boss of the menagerie got a new animal by express from Colorado when we were leaving Akron, O., and we got it in one end of a cage occupied by a happy family of rabbits, coons, a spotted leopard and a hound dog and a house cat. The new animal was a bob cat, such as Roosevelt shoots when the man has the camera ready to catch him in the act. Say, but that bob cat is a terror, and crosser than any animal we got, except the hyenas. The bob cat just walked around and snarled and spit at the happy family through the bars, and kept them awake all night on the road, and the happy family held a sort of convention and I could see by the way they all looked at me that they were passing resolutions inviting me to break up the bob cat business. The manager of the menagerie told pa he wished the confounded bob cat would escape, 'cause he was a blooming nuisance, so I thought I would help get rid of the beast, and save the show from disgrace. So when we got to Oberlin I thought that was a pious community that could stand a wild bob cat, so I put several sheets of sticky tanglefoot fly paper in the bob cat's cage and opened the door of the cage, after the crowd had gone into the main tent to the big show, and the menagerie tent was empty except the keepers. They were all asleep under the wagons, and the animals had all curled down for a nap, and the freaks were on their platform lolling around, waiting for the main show to be out so they could do their stunts over again.

The bob cat got all his four feet in the tanglefoot fly paper, then he grabbed a sheet in his mouth and rolled over in a few more sheets, and when he was entirely harmless and you couldn't tell what he was, I opened the door of the cage and he went out like a rocket, and rolled over a few times in the sawdust, and then jumped on the platform with the freaks, run over the fat woman, who was laying back in a Morris chair, and left one of the sheets of fly paper on her low neck, and it stuck like a porous plaster. She yelled that she had been stabbed, and pa came along just as the bob cat jumped off the platform, and struck pa on the back, and the cat spit at pa, and pa fell over among the sacred cattle and rolled under a cow and got on his knees, when the animals all began to roar, and pa crawled behind a bale of hay, and a zebra stepped on pa's face, and pa yelled "Hey, Rube," which is a grand hailing sign of distress when circus men want to fight, and about a hundred of the canvasmen came running with tent stakes to hit people with.

Pa crawled out from the bale of hay, which he had pulled over him, and the hay stuck to the fly paper on pa, and a camel began to eat the hay, and he chewed pa's shirt until the hands pulled pa away.

The bob cat escaped into the main tent, just as the Japanese jugglers were juggling in No. 1 ring, and the elephants were standing on their heads in No. 2 ring, and the flying trapeze artists were jumping from one trapeze to another, and the bob cat rushed through the Japanese, and amongst the elephants, with the fly paper all over him, and the audience fairly yelled, 'cause they thought it was a clown dressed up to do some stunt, but the Japanese left the ring in a panic, while the elephants got down off their heads and stood on their hind feet and cried like children.

The audience saw that something had happened that was serious and they all rose to their feet and were going off into a panic when pa and a few brave men came and drove the bob cat up a centerpole, away up above the torches, and made speeches to the audience, and quieted them down, and the performance went on. But pa was a sight, and the head circus man told pa he would have to dress better, or forever after hold his peace, and pa said if any man could be more patient than he was, with a bob cat on his neck, a sacred cow walking on him, and a camel trying to eat his whiskers and shirt, they better hire that man.

But it was all fixed up and everybody apologized to everybody, and the bob cat went on up the center pole and out on top of the canvas and escaped into Ohio, where it will probably be holding office before next fall.

Gee, but the giant is a coward. When the bob cat began to run up the giant's leg, and then up his back, and then jumped from his shoulder onto the fat lady, the giant turned pale and cried, and the midget said to him: "O, you big stiff, why didn't you have sand enough to hold the kitty till the keeper came? I've a good mind to get on a stepladder and kick you," and the cowardly giant cried again, and said if the midget ever struck him he would report him to the management. Just then pa came along and asked what the row was about, and when pa found that the midget was trying to pick a quarrel with the giant, he took the midget across his knee and gave him a few spanks, and told him to quit bullying the freaks. The midget got up on a barrel and called his son, who is bigger than pa, when I stepped in between them and told the midget's son if he struck my father I would have his heart's blood, and he quailed, and then I bullied the giant, who is a coward, and now they are all afraid of me.

I don't see how a big fellow like a giant can be afraid of things smaller than he is, and shy when a dog barks, and be afraid some one is going to smash him in the jaw, but pa says the size of a man don't make any difference, 'cause it is the heart that does the business. A man may be big enough and strong enough to tip over a box car, loaded with pig iron, but if his heart is one of these little ones intended for a miser, with no pepper sauce running from the heart to the arteries and things, and a liver that is white, and nerves that are trembly, and no gall to speak of, why a big man is liable to be walked all over by a nervy little man who is spunky, and gets mad and froths at the mouth.

I have been having great times with the monkeys, and I guess the manager will make me superintendent of monkeys, 'cause they all seem to be stuck on me, and will do anything I tell them to. Pa says they think I am some new kind of a monkey, and they look up to me. I lead out the big monkeys that ride the goats and dogs, and have a horse race in the ring, and fasten them on the little animals, and when they ride around the ring on the dogs and goats and ponies, they keep looking at me as though they wanted my approval.

There is one little monkey that sleeps nearly all the time, and I played a trick on pa with it that like to got me arrested and licked by a man who was mad. A man and woman with a baby in a little wagon were going through the menagerie, and it was crowded, and they left the baby and wagon in pa's charge, near the monkey cage, while they went to see the hippopotamus. Pa is the most accommodating man about holding babies that ever was. The baby was asleep when its folks left it in the wagon with pa, but it woke up while they were gone, and pa took it out of the baby wagon and carried it around just as he would at home, and showed it the animals, and held it up on his shoulder, and I took the little monkey and put it in the baby wagon, and it went to sleep, and I put a veil over it, and was standing by the wagon talking with a peanut butcher, when the parents of the baby came back, and the woman raised up the veil to see if the child was asleep, when the monkey woke up and put its hairy hands up to rub it eyes. The monkey looked up at the woman with beady eyes and began to chatter, and she yelled and her husband took a look at the monk, and he was mad. They could both see it was a monkey instead of a baby, and they asked where the old man with the chin whiskers was that they left the baby with, and the peanut butcher said: "What, that old guy with the checkered vest? Why, he has gone with the baby over to the lion cage, where they are feeding the lions. Don't you see him holding the baby upon his shoulder?" By ginger, I never saw two people sprint the way they did, 'cause I guess they thought pa was sure crazy, and would give the baby to the lions. But I told them the old man was all right, and would bring the baby back, and if he didn't they could have the monkey, 'cause I didn't want them to think they were going to be losers while attending our show. Then I chucked the monkey under the chin and said: "Maybe this is your baby, 'cause they change wonderfully when they get into a show."

Well, I just had time to put the monkey back in the cage when I saw that couple surround pa, and the woman grabbed the baby out of his arms, and the man tackled pa around the legs below the knee, and threw pa down under the ostrich cage, and said: "You kidnaper! I am a good mind to choke the life out of you," and he squeezed pa's windpipe until pa's tongue run out, when a canvasman came along and hit the man in the ear, and he laid down near a zebra, and the zebra kicked at the man and hit pa, 'cause a zebra is crosseyed and kicks like a woman throws a stone, and no man knows where it listeth.

Pa got up to murder the man that choked him, when the ostrich reached its head out between the bars of the cage and picked pa's big diamond stud off his shirt, big as a piece of rock candy, and swallowed it, and pa said that's the limit, and he called the manager and asked him how he was going to get his diamond stud out of the ostrich. The manager told pa to go to the dressing-room and ask the woman who has charge of the wardrobe for the ostrich stomach pump, and when he got the stomach pump the manager said the ostrich would cough up the diamond stud. Pa went off to the dressing-room to get the ostrich stomach pump, and I knew there was going to be trouble, 'cause I thought the manager was just stringing pa.

Well, he went up to the woman in the dressing-room, and said he came after her stomach pump, ostrich size, and you'd a died to see the ruction. The woman looked at pa as though he had escaped from a sanitarium, and then she seemed to think he was trying to make game of her, and she said: "You old skate, do you know who you have the honor of addressing? I am the queen of this realm, and they all kow-tow to me; now you come and take your medicine," and before pa could say boo she had pulled a big clothes bag over his head and tied it around his feet, and said: "Come on, girls, we are going to have roasted missionary," and they were lighting a gasoline torch to roast pa, when the owner of the show came along and asked what was up. When the wardrobe woman told him pa had insulted her, the owner gave her $10 to buy champagne for the performers, and she released pa, and he went back to choke his diamond out of the ostrich.

Pa says this life is more exciting, if anything, than staying at home, and it will either kill him or cure him of a desire to be a Barnum in about a month more.

CHAPTER VII.

The Circus Has a Yellow Fever Scare--The Bad Boy and His Dad Dress Up as Hottentots--Pa Takes a Mustard Bath and Attends a Revival Meeting.

Well, we have had a row for your life, and all the excitement anybody can stand. We got into Indiana and have had a yellow fever scare, a quarantine that lasted one night, so nobody could sleep on our train, a riot at Evansville 'cause we took on a couple of female trapeze women that came from Honduras, via New Orleans, and a revival of religion, all in one bunch, and pa is beginning to get haggard, like a hag.

The female trapeze performers, who had been expected ever since we started on the road, had been quarantined at New Orleans, where the yellow fever is raging, and finally got through the quarantine guard somewhere in Mississippi, and got to us Saturday afternoon, and some official telegraphed to the mayor that two yellow fever refugees had struck his town to join the circus, and he ordered the chief of police to hunt them out, and put them in a pest house. The Honduras females were yellow as saffron, but it was caused by the climate of Honduras, but the whole show was scared to death for fear we would all have yellow fever, and the management detailed pa and I to hide the yellow girls from the police.

Pa fixed up one of the cages, with the girls blacked up as Hottentots and pa and I blacked up as an African king and prince of the blood, and we did stunts in the cage at afternoon and evening performances, and the crowd could not keep away from our cage, until pa got hot and unbuttoned his shirt and, before we knew it, everybody saw pa's white skin below where his face and neck were blacked, and while we were talking gibberish to each other a country jake got mad and he led a crowd to open the cage and make us remove our shirts to prove that we were Hottentots.

When they found we were white people blacked up they wanted their money back and were going to tip over the cage, when pa saved the day by making a speech, at the evening performance, to the effect that we were all yellow fever refugees from New Orleans and the mob lit out on the run for the main tent, where they announced that there were four cases of fever in the menagerie tent, and that settled it.

The mayor and police closed the show on account of yellow fever, and we couldn't get out of the tent. Pa had been quite close to the yellow girls and when he found out that yellow fever was a disease that catches you when not looking, and in 15 minutes you look like a corpse, and in four hours you are liable to be a sure enough corpse, he shook the yellow girls, and asked an old sailor what a man ought to do who has been exposed to yellow fever, and the old sailor, who has had yellow fever lots of times, told pa to strip off his clothes and take a bath of prepared mustard, and rub it in thoroughly, and then wipe it off, and take a vinegar rub, and after that sprinkle a little red pepper on himself, put on different clothes and drink about a gallon of red lemonade and he could defy yellow fever.

Pa is an easy mark and he believed the old sailor, who is tattooed and makes a show of himself with the freaks, and pa took a change of clothes and a bottle of mustard and a cruet of vinegar and a bottle of red pepper and went into a dressing room and got behind a wagon and began to take the cure the sailor had prescribed. I don't know as it was right to do it, but about the time pa had got to the red pepper course and was sprinkling it on his skin pretty thick, and he was beginning to get pretty hot, and was yelling a little, I told the chief of police, who was looking around with the health officer for suspicious cases, that there was a man acting sort of queer behind the wagon that had a piece of canvas over the wheels. They both rushed in on pa and grabbed him.

Gee! but pa looked and smelled like a plate of pigs' feet and the doctor said it was an unmistakable case of yellow fever, he could tell by the smell, and then pa turned pale and yellow from fright, and they wrapped him up in a piece of canvas and took him away in an emergency hospital ambulance, and the whole show at once knew that we were in for a quarantine.

They burned up the suit of clothes pa took off and the one he was going to put on, and the ambulance drove away, while pa shook one fist at the sailor and one at me, and his skin began to shrink and smart, and he yelled, and the audience stampeded, and the show was in the dumps.

We had to stay over Sunday in Evansville, and the show people were so scared the manager thought he better have religious services in the tent Sunday, so they got a revivalist preacher to preach to them, a fellow who used to preach to the cowboys out west. Sunday morning the tough fellows in the show said they wouldn't do a thing to the preacher when he came on to do his stunt. Their idea was to wait until he got well on his sermon and then begin to interrupt him and ask questions, and finally to get a blanket and toss him up a few times for luck, and then chase him out and have the circus bulldog, that chews the clown's pants, catch the minister's coat tail and just scare him plum to death.

The boys said it would be the biggest picnic that ever was--a regular barbecue. The boss canvasman said he was opposed to mixing religion with the circus business, because the fellows could get all the religion they needed in the winter, when the show was laid up and he would see the boys through in anything they proposed to do to the sky pilot that was going to play his game in ring No. 1 at 10:30 the next day.

Well, after I heard the circus men talk about what they would do to the preacher, I was afraid they would kill him, so when he and a helper brought a little melodeon into the ring, facing the reserved seats, I told him the boys were going to raise a rumpus and drive him out of the tent with the bulldog hanging to his coat tails. He put his hand on his pistol pocket and pulled a long, blue gun about half way out, and let it drop back down beside his leg, and he winked at me and said he guessed not, scarcely, as he had preached to crowds so tough that a circus gang was a Sunday school in comparison.

Then I got on a front seat to watch the fun. About 800 of the circus hands, performers, clowns and peanut butchers, came in, snickering, and sat down on the reserved seats in front of the little pulpit, improvised from the barrels the elephants stand on, and some of them laughed and said: "Hello, Bill!" and "Ah, there!" and "Get on to his collar," and a lot of other things.

The little husky preacher had a Salvation Army girl to play the melodeon, and he didn't take any notice of the remarks the boys made, except to set his jaws together and moisten his lips. Finally they were all seated, and he got up to open the services, when a big canvasman, a regular Smart Aleck, got up on a seat and said: "Pardner, how you going to open this jack pot?"

The crowd laughed and the preacher pulled his long blue gun up out of his pocket, and laid it on the barrel, and then picked it up and pointed it at the big canvasman and said: "This game is going to be opened with this hand, seven of a kind, all 45 caliber, dum-dum bullets, and unless you sit down quick I will send a mess of bullets into your carcass right where your heart ought to be. If you open your mouth again before I say 'amen!' real loud at the close of the services, I will shoot all your front teeth out. Do you comprehend? If so, be seated."

The big fellow dropped on to the blue seat, as though he had been hit with a piledriver, and the crowd was so tickled to have the bully's bluff called, that they cheered the preacher. Then he said, "We will now open this jack pot with singing and I shall keep one eye on the gentleman who was last up, but who is now seated pretty low down."

You could have heard a pin drop.

The preacher wiped his face calmly, and said: "We will now sing and I expect every man will sing, and to that end I will appoint Big Ike, who asked me how I was going to open this jack pot, to come down in front of the seats and lead in the singing, for I know by his voice, which I heard in debate, that he is a crackerjack," and the preacher took hold of the handle of the blue gun and Big Ike walked down through the rows of seats, and as the melodeon began to squawk, Ike got down in front of the audience, and some of the boys said: "Bully for you, Ike," and after scratching his head a minute Ike turned and walked towards the preacher, at the edge of the ring, and I thought there was going to be the worst fight ever was, and as the preacher reached for the gun I crawled under the seat, and peeked out between the legs of a fat man, but Ike walked up to the minister and said, as the melodeon began to cough: "Boys, this tune is on Ike." He started it and every man sang.

When it was ended the boys clapped and stamped for an encore, and they sang it through again, and the face of the preacher beamed with joy, and I saw there was not going to be any fight and I crawled out from under the seats.

Pa came in the tent just then, with a new suit of clothes on, having been discharged from the hospital as cured of yellow fever, and I gave him my seat, and he held me in his lap.

The preacher then preached a sermon that did them all good. He dwelt upon the hard life of the showman, and gave them such good advice that when it was all over and he said he wanted to shake hands with every man in the bunch, Ike marshaled them all up to the ring and introduced them, and no minister ever was more cordially congratulated, and they wanted him to go along with the show, and preach every Sunday.

The preacher said he couldn't join the show, but he traveled around a good deal and he would probably be in the same town with the show several times during the summer and he would drop in on them occasionally and keep them straight.

Pa was watching the crowd for the sailor who prescribed cayenne pepper for yellow fever, and when he saw the sailor come up to the minister, with tears in his eyes, and say: "Parson, I has been a bad man and killed a man once, but he was a Portuguese sailor, and he had the drop on me, the same as you did on Big Ike at the opening of these proceedings, and I had to kill him. And I begs the pardon of this old gentleman for lying to him." And then pa shook hands with the sailor and the parson, and the parson put his blue gun down his trousers leg, and said: "By the way, the bulldog you were going to let take a lunch off me, is he all right?"

Then the parson and the girl went away, and the boys carried out the melodeon, and the quarantine was declared off. After dinner the boys took down the tents and put them on the train that Sunday afternoon, singing decent songs as they pulled up the stakes and rolled up the canvas, and on the train, late in the night, we could hear "Old Hundred" being sung as the cars ran through the pennyrial district of Indiana.

CHAPTER VIII

Pa Takes the Place of the Fat Woman with Disastrous Results--A
Kentucky Colonel Causes a Row--Pa Tries to Roar Like a Lion and the
Rhinoceros Objects--Pa Plays the Slot-Machine and Gets the Worst of
It.

This has been an eventful week with the show. We have had heat prostrations in Kentucky, nearly the whole show got drunk on 16-year-old whisky, and if it hadn't been for the animals keeping sober this show would have been pulled for disorderly conduct.

Nobody knows how the row started, but pa says every man in Kentucky carries a blue gun and a bottle of red licker, and they wear white hats, so the red, white and blue business is all right, only it is a combination that is death on a circus. I think one of the ushers, at the afternoon performance, told an old colonel that he must move along quicker, when the colonel began to talk back, and say, "Who is you talkin' too, sah?" And the usher stood it as long as he could, when he took the colonel by the collar and sat him down so quick he didn't come to for a couple of minutes, and when the colonel got his senses, and found that the usher had ushered him into a seat between two gaily decorated colored women the trouble began. The colonel never forgot that he was a gentleman, for he rose up, took off his hat to the colored women, and said: "You must excuse me, ladies, but I shall have to go and kill the scoundrel who sat me down with niggers," and he got down off the seats and struck the usher with his cane, and the usher yelled: "Hey, Rube!" and all the circus people made a rush for the colonel. The colonel said, "Men of Kentucky, to the rescue," and before I could crawl under the seats the air was full of baggage, seats, tent pins and white hats, guns were fired, and blood flowed, and the police pulled everybody, and the evening performance was given up.

One of the proprietors of the show got a wen on his head as big as a football from being struck by a handle of a revolver, and the colonel who started the row was knocked silly by a tray of red lemonade which the butcher smashed him with, and the colonel cried because the lemonade was all water, and he was afraid it would soak into him and cause him to warp. When the lemonade butcher apologized, and the usher told him it was all a mistake his being seated with the niggers, the colonel wept on their necks and invited the whole crowd to go to his distillery and help themselves.

When we got to the next town every man in the show had a grouch and a Katzenjammer, and their hair was so sore it was murder and suicide combined to comb it.

The way pa escaped injury was 'cause he had to take the place of the fat woman on the platform with the freaks, as the fat woman was overcome with the heat and had to stay in the car.

The way they fixed pa up to resemble the fat woman was scandalous. They have some rubber things in the wardrobe tent that you can blow up and make a big arm, and a big leg, and a big stummick, so anybody couldn't tell the difference, and they fixed pa up with blowed up clothes of flesh colored rubber, and but for his chin whiskers you couldn't tell him from the fat woman. He said he wouldn't cut off his whiskers for anybody's circus, so they fixed a veil to cover part of his face and put the fat woman's dress on pa, and put him up beside the skeleton, the midget and the giant.

Pa said he didn't want to do it, 'cause it seemed too much like fraud, but they told him the fate of the show depended on our all being willing to take any part assigned to us, and so pa sat down and began to fan himself, and tried to look flirty like a woman.

The other freaks never noticed but what it was the fat woman until the show was half over. It was too much for me, and I just laffed at pa. I got up behind him and told him in a whisper that I wanted a dollar to play the slot machine, and he told me to go to thunder, and get out of there. I couldn't stand it to be insulted by my own father, so I took a hat pin out of the hat of the bearded lady and punched it into pa's blowed up rubber shirt, and pa began to sis, like a soda fountain, and the wind struck the living skeleton and blew him over like a cyclone, and by that time pa was blowing off wind in a dozen places that I had punctured, and he was scared for fear there wouldn't be anything left of him, and the giant saw the fat woman slowly fading away, and the coward had heart failure and lay down on the platform. Somebody shouted that the fat woman was all melting away, and a fellow who was watering a camel out of a bucket came to the rescue and threw the bucket of dirty water all over pa, and then I thought I better go away into the tent and see the fight, but pa was taken to the dressing room and rescued from the shrinking rubber balloons that were busted, and he said he would hunt the man that punctured his tire to his dying day, but he didn't know it was me.

Gee, it looks to me as though pa has been engaged to act as the easy mark in this show. Say, they got pa to practice on roaring like a lion, so he could stand behind the cage when the lion has a sore throat and roar, and scare folks, and pa has been going around behind the cages, every evening, when the menagerie is closed, and the crowd in the main tent, making noises that have made the animals look at each other as much as to say, "Well, what do you think of that?" The rhinoceros was so disgusted at Paducah that he reached out his nose and took pa on his horn and held him up to the scorn of the other animals until pa's pants gave way and he was a sight, and he was so scared that he got out of the tent and made a run for our train, chased by the police, who thought he was a burglar that had been eat by a house dog.

The worst thing we have had on pa was at Louisville, where we stayed over Sunday. Another fellow and I got a system on slot machines, and one day we beat the machines out of a shotbag full of nickels, and when we showed up at the tent all the fellows wanted to know how we did it, and pa said it was gambling, and we ought not to do it, but he also wanted to know how we managed to win, and when we told pa about it pa said it was no sin to beat a slot machine, 'cause it was an inanimate thing, just a machine, and anybody who could beat a nickel in the slot machine at his own game was equal to a Rockefeller.

So after everybody had got excited about our nickels I told them how to beat the machine. I told them I didn't get excited and go rushing in where angels fear to tread, and feed the slot machine on good hard earned nickels of my own, but waited until the countrymen and tenderfeet had fed it on nickels until it was too full for utterance. When the machine swelled out like it was blowed up, and it kind of wheezed, like it was ready to cough up, and was only waiting for an excuse, I put a cough lozenger about the size of a nickel in the slot and turned the diaphram. The machine shuddered a minute and then had a regular hemorrhage, and coughed up a tin cupful of nickels into my hand, and the machine seemed to rest easy, and take nourishment again from the silly fellows, who thought they could beat it.

Well, sir, the whole crowd was so excited they could hardly wait to find a slot machine, and finally they bought nearly all my cough lozengers, and went out into the night, and pa and I went along, 'cause pa said he understood all the slot machines were owned by Rockefeller, and he made more money on them than he did on Standard oil, and the money that he gave away to schools and churches was from his rake-off on his slot machines. Pa said it would be a good thing if someone could break up the reprehensible practice by beating the blasted machines to a finish.

So pa he got a bag to bring back the nickels in, and a bunch of us went to a store where one whole side of the place was filled with slot machines, and the way the people were playing the game was scandalous. Pa watched a machine until the players had fed it so it seemed as though it would die unless it got air, and he stepped up and put in a lozenger and turned the wheel, and held the bag under the spout for the coin, but it didn't come. Some more fellows put in nickels, and the machine gave little hacking coughs and coughed up three or four nickels, but nothing that seemed at all in the nature of a financial hemorrhage, when pa took another lozenger and put it in, and by ginger the machine began to heave up nickels like it was in the trough of the sea.

Pa was so excited he forgot to hold the bag, and nickels went all over the floor, and everybody made a grab for them, and pa was shoved aside, and he swore he would have the place pulled, and just then a law officer took pa in charge because he had put a cough lozenger in the slot machine, and he searched pa and found a lot more bronchial trochees, and pa was in for it on a charge of malpractice, for giving cough medicine for the stomach trouble of the slot machine, instead of pepsin tablets.

They took pa in a back room and searched him some more, and found his roll, and then a man who said he was a lawyer offered to help pa, and keep him out of the penitentiary. He told pa the law of Kentucky made the crime of trifling with a slot machine the same as breach of promise, or arson, and that he would be lucky if he got off with ten years in the pen, with 30 days' solitary confinement in a Turkish bath cell, with niggers for companions.

Pa turned blue and asked the lawyer if there was no way out of it, and the lawyer told him that for $120 in spot cash he would let him go, and fight the case after the show had got out of the state. A hundred and twenty-five dollars was the amount they found on pa, and he told them that inasmuch as they already had it, they better keep the money and let him go, and he would be always a living example of the terrors of gambling.

So they let pa go, and all the way to the train he told us he hoped this experience would be a lesson to us not to covet the money of the rich, and as far as he was concerned, John D. Rockefeller could go plum to thunder with his money after this.

Then we got to the car, and found about a dozens of the circus men who had been out to beat the slot machines, broke flat, and I had to divide my shot bag of nickels with them, that I had won before I let them into the game, before they would let me go to bed.

Dad says this circus life is making me pretty tough.

CHAPTER IX.

The Bad Boy Feeds Cayenne Pepper to the Sacred Cow--He and His Pa
Ride in a Circus Parade With the Circassian Beauties--A Tipsy
Elephant Lands Them in a Public Fountain--Pa Makes the Acquaintance
of John L. Sullivan.

I am learning more about animals every day, and when the season is over I will be an expert animal man. Animals naturally have a language of their own, and lions understand each other, and bears can converse with bears, but in a show, all animals seem to have a common language, so they understand each other a little.

I found that out when I put a paper of cayenne pepper into a head of lettuce and gave it to the sacred cow. She chewed the lettuce as peacefully as could be, and swallowed the cayenne pepper, and then stopped to think. You could tell by the expression on her face that when the pepper began to heat her up inside she wanted to swear, although she was a sacred cow. She humped herself, and shivered, and then bellowed like a calf who has been left in the barn to be weaned, while its mother goes out to pasture, and the sacred bull, her husband, he came and put his nose up to her nose, as much as to say: "What is the matter, dearie?" and she talked sacred cattle talk to him for a minute, and then the bull turned to me and chased me out of the tent. Now, as sure as you live that cow told the bull that I had given her something hot. All the animals within hearing were onto me, and they would snarl, and make noises when I came along, and act as though they wanted to make me understand that they knew I gave that cow a hot box, and they all wanted to get a chance at me.

They don't like pa any better than they do me, and the big elephant seems to have been laying for pa ever since he run the sharp iron into him, the time he got on a tear and tried to run a town. When the elephants are performing in the ring, they all have an eye on pa, so everybody notices it. I knew something would happen to pa, so when the man who plays the sheik, and rides the elephant in the street parade, in a howdah, with a canopy over it, with some female houris in it, and they called for a volunteer to do the sheik act, at Steubenville, and pa offered to do the stunt, I went along as an Egyptian girl, 'cause I knew there would be something doing.

The elephant eyed pa when he got up into the bungalow on top of him with the Circassian woman and me, and winked at the other elephants, as much as to say: "Watch my smoke." As he went out from the lot, on the way downtown, ahead of the bunch, all the other animals acted peculiar, and seemed to say: "He will get his before we get through this parade."

The big elephant is one of the best ring performers, but he has always been steady in the street parade, with the light of Asia on his back. We got to the edge of town and stopped to let the rear wagons close up, and were in front of a saloon, where the bartender had been emptying stale beer out of the bottoms of kegs into a washtub, which was standing on the sidewalk, ready to be sold to people who buy it in pails.

Well, sir, that confounded elephant got his trunk in that tub of stale beer, and he never took it out till the beer was all gone. I looked down from the pagoda and told pa the elephant was drinking again, and had drank a washtub of beer, but pa couldn't say anything, 'cause he was doing the Arab sheik act, and had to look dignified, as though he was praying to Allah.

But just then the band struck up, and we started down the main street of Steubenville. The people began to cheer, 'cause our elephant began to hippity-hop, and waltz sideways across the street and back again, and I thought pa would die. In the parade one man on a horse attends to the elephants, so the sheiks don't have anything to say, and pa remained like a statue, and told me and the Circassian beauties to be calm, and trust in him and Allah. This Allah business was all right when the elephant waltzed, but when we got to the next block the beast began to stand on his hind feet, and pa and the houris rolled to the back end of the howdah, and were all piled in a heap, while I held on to the cloth of gold over the elephant's head.

Pa yelled to the people on horseback to kill the elephant, and the crowd cheered, thinking it was the best performance they ever saw in a free street parade, and the animals in the cages behind were yapping as though they knew what was going on. The elephant got down on all fours, and we straightened up in the pagoda, and for a block or so the beast only waltzed around. As we got to some sort of a public square, where there were thousands of people, the stale beer seemed to be getting in its work, for the elephant looked at the people, as much as to say: "Now I will show you something not down on the bills," and, by ginger, if he didn't raise up his hind quarters and stand on his front feet, right by the side of a big fountain, and he reached in his trunk for a drink, when all of us on the pagoda clung to pa, and we all slid right off into the big basin of water. The fountain played on us, and pa was under water, with the four Circassian beauties, and when we rolled or slid down over the elephant's head, he looked at us and seemed to chuckle: "What you getting off here for, the show ain't half out."

Well, the parade went on and left the elephant and the rest of us at the fountain, and to show that animals understand each other, and can appreciate a joke, every animal that passed us gave us the laugh, even the hippopotamus, which opened his mouth as big as a tunnel, and showed his teeth and acted as though he would like to exchange tanks with us.

The circus people that could be spared from the wagons came to help us, and the citizens helped out the Circassian beauties who were praying to Allah, and wringing out their clothes, and I crawled up on the neck of a cast-iron swan in the fountain. Pa yelled and talked profane, and told 'em to bring a cannon and kill the elephant, which kept ducking him with his trunk, and swabbing out the bottom of the fountain basin with pa. It seemed as though he never would get through using pa for a mop, but finally the people got a rope around pa, and a keeper got an iron hook in the elephant's ear, and they pulled pa out on one side, and got the elephant away on the other side, and just then the callipoe, that ends the parade, came by us and played the "Blue Danube," and the elephant got on his hind feet and waltzed on the pavement. They put pa and the Circassian beauties in a patrol wagon and took them to the show lot, and I sat by the driver, and he let me drive the team.

Pa had his sheik clothes rolled up around his waist, and was wringing them out, and talking awful sassy, and when we got to the lot it took a long time to convince the policemen that we were not guilty of disorderly conduct, and just then the elephant came tearing by us, with the keeper on horseback behind him, prodding him in the ham every jump with a sharp iron, and he went through the side of the tent as though he was mighty sorry he didn't kill us all.

They made him get down on his knees and bellow in token of surrender, and then we all went and changed our clothes for the afternoon performance. As we passed through the menagerie tent, dripping, every animal set up a yell, as much as to say: "There, maybe you will give cayenne pepper to a pious sacred cow again, confound you," and that convinces me that animals are human.

The last week has been the hardest on pa of any week since we have been out with the circus. The trouble with pa is that he wants to be "Johnny on the spot," as the boys say, and if anything breaks he volunteers to go to work and fix it, and if anybody is sick or disabled, he wants to take their place, as he says so he will learn everything about the circus, and be competent to run a show alone next year.

But it was a mean trick the principal owner of the show played on pa at Canton, O. You see John L. Sullivan used to do a boxing act with this show, years ago, and everybody likes John, and when he shows up where the show gives a performance he has the freedom of the whole place, and everybody about the show is ready to fall over themselves to do John L. a service.

Well, Sullivan showed up at Canton, and he went everywhere, all the forenoon, and met all the old timers, and at the afternoon performance he was awfully jolly.

John was standing beside the ring when the Japanese jugglers were juggling, and he leaned against a pole. Pa came in from the menagerie tent, and he didn't know Sullivan, and when he saw Sullivan holding the pole up, pa said to the boss proprietor that the fat man who was interfering with the show ought to be called down or put out.

The boss said to pa: "You go take him by the ear and put him out," and pa, who is as brave as lion, started for Sullivan, and the boss winked at the other circus men, and pa went up to Sullivan and took hold of John's neck with both hands, and said: "Come on out of here."

Well, sir, we ought to have moving pictures of what followed. Sullivan turned on pa, and growled just like a lion. Then he took pa around the waist and held him up under his arm, and picked up a piece of board and slatted pa just as though pa was a child, and the audience just yelled, and pa called to the circus men for help, but they just laughed.

Pa got a chance at the fat man and he hit him in the jaw, but it did not hurt Sullivan, only made him mad. He took pa up by the collar and whirled him around until pa was dizzy, and then he started with him for the menagerie tent, and called to the boss canvasman: "Bill, come on and tell me which is the hungriest lion, and I will feed him with this cold meat."

Pa yelled, 'cause he thought he was in the hands of an escaped lunatic, and the circus hands came and took him away. Then the owner told pa who Sullivan was, and pa almost fainted. But finally, after breathing hard for awhile, pa went up to Sullivan and shook his hand, and said: "Mr. Sullivan, you must excuse me. If I had known you were the great John L., I would not have licked you." Sullivan looked at pa and said: "Well, you are a wonder, old man, and you did do me up," and pa and Sullivan became great friends. Since then pa is pretty chesty, 'cause the circus men point him out to the jays as the man who whipped John L. Sullivan.

CHAPTER X.

The Bad Boy and His Pa Drive a Roman Chariot--They Win the Race, but
Meet With Difficulties--The Bearded Lady to the Rescue--A Farmer's
Cart Breaks Up the Circus Procession.

Ohio was a hoodoo for the circus business, and Kentucky got the whole
bunch ready for a long stay at Dwight, Ill., but the agent routed us into
Pennsylvania, and pa has had nothing but a series of disasters since
striking the state.

Pa gave notice that when we got to his old home, at Scranton, where he lived
when he was a boy, he wanted to sort of run things, so his old neighbors would see
that he had got up in the world since he left the old town. So the manager gave pa
about 400 free tickets to distribute among his friends, and arranged for pa to show
off as the leading citizen in the show. He was offered a chance to take the place of
the clown, the ring master or anybody whose duty he thought he could perform. Pa
selected the place of driver of the Roman chariot with four horses abreast, in place
of the Irish Roman who was accustomed to drive the chariot in the race with the
female charioteer, a muscular girl who used to clerk in a livery stable at Chicago.

The chariot race is a fake, because it is arranged for the girl to win, so the audience will go wild and cheer her, so she has to come bowing all around the ring. The
way the job is put up is for the two chariots to start, and go around twice. On the
first turn the man driver is ahead, and takes the pole, and on the second turn the
girl's ahead, and she takes the pole, and on the third turn the man is ahead, and they
begin to whip the horses, who seem crazy, and on the last stretch the man holds
his team back a little, and the girl passes him and comes out a trifle ahead, and the
crowd goes wild.

Well, the master of ceremonies coached pa about the business, and told him what to do. They knew he could drive four horses, because he said he was an old stage driver, and when he got in the chariot with the Roman suit on gleaming with gold, and the brass helmet, and the cloth of gold gauntlets, and stood up like a senator, gee, I was proud of him, and when he and the female drove out of the dressing-room and halted by the door for the announcer to announce the great Ben Hur chariot race, I got into the chariot behind pa, and told him he must win the race, or the people of Scranton would mob him. For they knew these races were usually fixed beforehand, but since he was to drive one of the teams, all his friends were betting on him, and if he pulled the team and let that livery stable lady win the race, they would accuse him of giving free tickets to get them in the show and skin them out of their money.

Pa said to me: "This race is going to be on the square, and you watch my smoke. Do you think I would let that red-headed dish washer beat me? Not on your life."

The play is to have a little boy kiss the male driver good-by, and a little girl kiss the female driver good-by, as though they were taking their lives in their hands. I had climbed up to pa and put my arms around his neck, and kissed him, and a girl kissed the female, when the gong sounded, and both four-horse teams made a jump, before I could get out of the chariot, so I got right in front of pa and peeked over the dashboard of the chariot, and, gee, but didn't we fairly whizz by the poles, and the audience looked like a panorama.

Pa got the pole and kept it, and we went around three times, and found the female chariot ahead of us, cause pa had gone around twice to her once. She turned out a little right by the band-stand, and pa run his team right inside her chariot and caught her wheel, and when he yelled to his team, her cart, team, and all were thrown right into the band, which scattered over the backs of the seats. The horses were all mixed up with the instruments, and the female driver was thrown into the air and came down in a sitting position right into the bass drum. She went right through the sheepskin, so her head and hands and feet were all of her that remained outside the drum.

She yelled for help and the circus hands rolled the drum, with her in it, into the dressing-room, where they had to cut the sides of the drum with an ax, to get her out, while others caught her horses and pulled the chariot out of the band, and the music stopped; but pa went on forever.

He went around six times yelling like an Indian at a green corn dance, and when he thought it was time to let up, because he had missed the other chariot, he pulled so hard he broke the lines on the two inside horses and then it was a runaway for sure, and the audience stood up on the seats and yelled, and women fainted.

Finally the circus hands grabbed some hurdles, and threw them across the track, near the main entrance, and when we came around the last time, two of the horses jumped the hurdles all right, but two fumbled and fell down, and there was a crash, and I didn't know anything until I felt cold water on my face that tasted sour, and colored my shirt red, and I found the lemonade butcher was bringing me to by pouring a tray of lemonade over me.

When my eyes opened, I saw a sight that I shall never forget. It seems that when the horses fell down, the chariot and the other two horses and pa and I had landed all in a heap right on top of the lemonade and peanut concession, and carried it up onto a row of seats near the main entrance from the menagerie. The elephants that were to come on next were in the door waiting for their signal, and they were scared at the crash, and they came in bellowing, the keepers having lost all control of them. The audience was stampeding, and the circus men were trying to straighten things out.

Pa struck on his head against a wagon wheel and his brass helmet was driven down over his face, so when he yelled to be pulled out of the helmet his voice sounded like a coon song, coming from a phonograph. It was the closest call from death pa ever had, 'cause they had to cut the helmet with a can opener to let pa out, like you open a can of lobsters. When they got the helmet opened so pa could come out, he looked just like a boiled lobster, and when the chief owner of the circus came up on a run, and asked if pa was dead, pa said: "Not much, Mary Ann; did I win?" and the manager said it was a pity they ever opened that helmet and let pa out. The man told pa he won in a walk, but the chief of police of Scranton was going to arrest pa for exceeding the speed limit.

They took pa to the dressing-room on a piece of board, and when the woman driver saw him, she got an ax, and wanted to cleave him from head to foot, but the bearded woman stepped in front of her and said: "Not on your life," and she shielded pa from death with her manly form, which pa says he shall never forget. Pa's old friends in Scranton gave him a banquet that night, but pa couldn't eat anything, cause the rim of the brass helmet cut a gash in his Adam's apple.

After the chariot race the managers concluded they wouldn't let pa have any position of importance again very soon, and I made up my mind you wouldn't ever catch me in any game that pa was in; but in the circus business you can never tell what is going to happen from one day to another.

On the train on the way to Wilkes Barre there was a hot box on one of the sleepers, and the car was side-tracked all night.

When we arrived at the town about 40 wagon drivers that were in the car did not show up, and they had to press everybody that could drive a team into the service to haul the stuff to the lot, and pa drove four horses so well with a load of tent poles that the manager complimented pa, and that gave pa the big head. When the parade was all ready to start through town, and the drivers had not arrived, the manager asked pa if he thought he could drive the ten gray horses on the band wagon, to lead the procession, and pa said driving ten horses was his best hold, and he got up on the driver's seat, and called me to get up with him, and I hate a boy that will disobey a parent, so I climbed up and began to jolly the band about the chariot race, and I told them pa wouldn't do a thing to them this time.

The manager of the show always rides ahead of the parade, with the chief of police of the town, and the band horses follow him, so it is easy enough to drive ten horses, cause all you have to do it to hold on to the 20 lines, and look savage at the crowd on the sidewalks, and the horses go right along, and the people think the driver is a wonder. So when the manager started in his buggy pa pulled up on all the lines he could hold on to, which filled his lap, and made him look like a harness maker, and he yelled: "Ye-up," and the procession moved, and the ten teams pa was driving went along all right, and pa looked as though he owned the show and the town.

We got downtown, to a wide street, and there was a fire alarm ahead, or something, and the procession stopped, and the manager and chief of police disappeared, and there was a wagon load of green corn stalks right beside the lead team, which a farmer was taking to a silo, but he had stopped his team to see the parade. The three teams of pa's leaders, six horses, began to eat the corn stalks, and the camels, that were behind us, worked along up by the band wagon and began to eat, and the farmer got scared to see his corn stalks disappearing, so he drove off on a side street, and started for the silo, and by ginger, pa's team turned onto the side street and followed the wagon of corn stalks, and pa couldn't hold them, and the band played, "In the Good Old Summer Time, There Will Be a Hot Time in the Old Town."

The camels kept up with the farmer's wagon, too, and the whole parade followed the band. The farmer started his horses into a run, and the team of ten horses that was driving pa started to galloping, and I looked back, and the elephants were beginning to gallop, and all the cages were coming whooping, and it was a picnic. The band stopped playing, and the players were scared, and as we were crossing a little bridge over a small stream, on the edge of town, I turned around to the band and told them to jump for their lives, and they all made a jump for the stream, and the air was full of uniforms and instruments, and they landed in the stream all right.

We went on up a hill, and were in the country, and the farmer turned into a farmyard, and the band wagon followed, and the farmer jumped off the corn stalk wagon and rushed for the house, and pa's ten-horse team surrounded the wagon, and every horse was eating corn stalks, and the team was all mixed up. The camels and the elephants crowded in for the nice green lunch, and the farmer's wife came out with her apron waving, and said "Shoo," but none of the animals shooed worth a cent, and pa pulled on the lines, and yelled, while the rest of the parade came into the farm and lined up. The drivers yelled at pa to know where in thunder he was going, and pa said: "Damfino."

Just then the manager and chief of police came up, and the way they talked to pa was awful. Pa couldn't explain how it was that he took the parade out in the country, and you never saw such a time.

By this time the regular drivers had arrived on a special, from where we left them with a hot box, and they took possession of the teams, and we got back to the circus lot in time for the afternoon performance. I don't know what they are doing to pa, but they had him in the manager's tent all the afternoon with some doctors, who seem to be examining him for insanity.

Everybody about the show thinks pa has hoodooed the aggregation, but pa says such things are always happening, and it is wrong to blame him.

The farmer got paid for his corn stalks, and it is to be charged up to pa.

CHAPTER XI.

The Bad Boy and His Pa in a Railroad Wreck--Pa Rescues the "Other Freaks"--They Spend the Night on a Meadow--A Near-Sighted Claim Agent Settles for Damages--Pa Plays Deaf and Dumb and Gets Ten Thousand.

It has come at last.

Everybody about the show expects that the show has got to have a railroad wreck every season, and all hands lay awake nights on the cars to brace themselves for the shock. Sometimes it comes early in the season, and again a show goes along until almost the end of the season without a shake-up, and fellows think maybe there is not going to be any wreck, but the engineers are only waiting till everybody has forgotten about it, and then, biff, bang, and they have run into another train, or been run into, and you have to be pulled out of a window by the heels, and laid out in a marsh until the claim agents can settle with you.

I always thought in reading of railroad accidents, that the railroad sent out a special trainload of doctors and nurses, to care for the injured, but the special train never has a doctor until the lawyers give first aid to the wounded in the way of financial poultices for the cripples. People in our business are on the railroads, and we work them for all there is in it; and the man that is hurt the least makes the biggest howl, and gets the biggest slice of indemnity. Some circus people spend all their salary as they go along, and live all winter on the damages they get from the railroads when the wreck comes.

The night of the wreck our train was whooping along at about 90 miles an hour, on a hippity-hop railroad in Pennsylvania, and the night was hot, and the mosquitoes from across the line in New Jersey were singing their solemn tunes, and pa, who attended a lodge meeting that night at the town we showed in, was asleep and talking in his sleep about passwords and grips, and the freaks and trapeze performers in our car had got through kicking about how the show was running into the ground, when suddenly there was a terrific smash-up ahead, an engine boiler exploded, a freight car of dynamite on a side track exploded and there was a grinding and bumping of cars. Then they rolled down a bank, over and over, so the upper berth was the lower berth half the time, and finally the whole business stopped in a hay marsh, and the bilge water in the marsh leaked into the hold of our car; people screamed, and some one yelled "fire!" and I pulled on pa till he woke up.

I thought pa's head was all caved in, because he talked nutty. The first thing he said was: "Say I, pronounce your name, and repeat after me," and then he said: "I promise and swear that I will never reveal the secrets of this degree," and then the conductor pulled pa's leg and said: "Crawl out of the window, old man, 'cause the train is in the ditch, the car is afire, and if you don't get out in about a minute with the other freaks, you will be a burnt offering."

Pa said you couldn't fool him, 'cause he knew he was being initiated into the 20-steenth degree of the Masons, and he guessed he could tell a degree from a train wreck, 'cause the degree was a darn sight worse than a wreck, but the conductor took one of those long glass fire extinguishers and sprinkled the medicated water on the freaks in the next berth, and then turned it on pa, and pa tasted it, and thought he was at a banquet, and he said "that sauterne is not fit to drink."

Then when the bearded woman yelled that the fire had almost reached her whiskers, and would nobody save her, pa began to get ready to move on, 'cause he concluded he hadn't been riding a goat after all, and he told me to hand him his pants. Pa is a man that will never go out among people, no matter how dark the night is, without his pants, and I admire him for it. Some of the circus men didn't care for dress that night, but got out just as they were, and the result was that when daylight came they had to tie hay around their legs.

Our car was bottom-side up, but I found pa's pants and he got his legs in, and I buttoned him in, but I felt all the time as though I had buttoned them in the back, so the seat was in front, but the fire was crackling and pa pushed me out of a transom, and then he crawled out, and we sat down in the mud.

The bearded woman came next, with her whiskers done up in curl papers, and then the fat woman got one foot through the transom, and she couldn't get it back in, and the train hands got an ax and were going to cut her leg off, and save one foot, at least, when pa got a move on him, and took the ax and broke out the side of the car, and got her out. Eight or nine men lifted her tenderly onto a stack of hay, and she wrapped it around her, 'cause she left her clothes in her berth.

Well, it was a sight when the people were got out of our car, and they let it burn, to light up the scene, and pa and I and the boss canvasman went along the ditched train, and helped people out. The giant was in two upper berths, and he got one leg out of the transom over one berth, and one leg out of the transom over the other berth, and we pulled his legs, but he couldn't make it, so pa took an ax and made both berths into one, and got him out.

The giant shook himself and started on a run across the marsh, but he mired up to his neck, and a farmer who heard the noise came to order us off his hay field for trespass, and yelled: "Here's a head of some of your performers cut off away over here," and he was going to bring it in, when the farmer found the head was alive, and he ran away from it.

In an hour we had everybody out, and made beds for them by spreading out hay cocks, and nobody seemed to be hurt so very much. We heard a locomotive whistle up the road, and some one said the relief train was coming with doctors and nurses, but the show owner who was with us said: "Relief doctors, nothing. That is a train-load of lawyers and claim agents to settle with us. The doctors will not come till to-morrow. Now, everybody pretend to be hurt awful bad, and strike the sharks for $10,000 apiece, and come down to $100, if you can't do any better."

It was getting daylight, and the relief train stopped, and the good Samaritans came wading into the hay marsh, bent on settling with us cheap. The first lawyer asked the principal owner how many were killed, 'cause they could figure exactly how much they have to pay for a dead one, but the live ones are the ones that make trouble for a railroad, 'cause they can kick and argue. The boss said nobody was dead, but the giant, who was mired in out of sight. The giant heard what was said, and he yelled that he was alive, and wouldn't settle for less than $20,000, but the claim agent said the giant would be dead in 15 minutes in that quicksand, so he would let him sink, and pay for him as a dead one.

The giant said if they would pull him out of the mud he would settle for $100, and they pulled him out, and the rest of the injured were going to mob him for settling so cheap.

One of the claim agents found the bearded woman sitting on a hay cock, combing out her whiskers, and asked what it would take to settle, and she said $10,000, and she got up and walked over to another hay cock where the Circassian beauty was drying her hair, and the claim agent looked at how spry the bearded woman walked, and he said to the boss: "I won't give that fellow with the curly whiskers a single kopeck," and the bearded woman came back and swatted the claim agent for calling her a fellow. So they compromised on $200, and she went behind the haystack and put it in her stocking, which convinced the claim agent that she wasn't a man.

A near-sighted claim agent came to the haystack where the fat woman was, and the boss told her now was her time to have a mess of hysterics, so she set up a cry that scared the agent, who thought there were at least six women on the haystack, and he said: "What will all of you people up there on the haystack settle for in a lump, for I am in a hurry?"

The fat woman caught on at once, and said: "We will all settle for $10,000." Then she yelled, and the agent thought her back was broke, and he offered $7,500, and she cried and said: "Make it $10,000," and the agent said: "I will go you," and he made out a check, and the fat woman had some more hysterics.

I had watched the settling all around, and I told pa to be deaf and dumb when they came to him, and just point to the seat of his pants in front and buttoned up behind, and look as though he was suffering the tortures of the inquisition, and let me do the talking, and I would make the old railroad go into a receiver's hands.

So pa said: "You are the boss," and he looked so pitiful that I almost cried.

When the near-sighted claim agent came to pa, I told him that pa's last words were to beg to be shot, and the man looked at pa's pants, and then at his face, and said: "What hit him? That's the worst case I ever saw in a railroad wreck."

I put my handkerchief to my eyes and said: "Well, when the shock came, pa was all right, as handsome a man as you would often see. I think there must have been a pile driver on the train that struck him, and changed sides with him, knocking his stomach around on the back side of him, and placing his spinal column around in front of him, where his stomach was, and causing him to lose the sense of speech. Think of a middle-aged man going through life mixed up in that manner, having to sit down on his stomach, and having his backbone staring him in the face. How does he know when he takes food in his mouth that it can corkscrew around under his arm and eventually find his stomach? How a man can be ground and twisted, and mauled, and stamped on by a reckless locomotive with a crazy engineer and a drunken fireman, rolled over by box cars, and walked on by elephants, and still live, is beyond me. As he told me before he lost the power of speech, not to be too hard on the railroad company, though some railroads would be glad to pay him $20,000, and no questions asked, he begged me, as heir to his estate, to let you off for a paltry $10,000."

Pa made up the darndest face, and groaned. The agent called another agent, and they whispered together, and finally the first one came to me and asked pa's full name, and then the two of them got out a fountain pen, and they made out a check, and he said: "This is the first case in the history of railroad wrecking that the agent has not had the heart to try to beat the injured party down. This is certainly the most pitiful case that has ever been known, and if your father ever comes to his senses you can tell him he is welcome to the money."

The agents shook hands with pa and I, and went away to their train, and pa winked at me, and a wrecking train came and we got on a special, and got to Pittsburg before breakfast, and pa is going to buy me a dog out of the money.

Gee, but there is all kinds of money in the circus business. Pa is going to wear his pants hind side before until we get out of Pittsburg.

CHAPTER XII.

The Bad Boy Causes Trouble Between the Russian Cossacks and the Jap Jugglers--A Jap Tight-Rope Walker Jiu-Jitsu's Pa--The Animals Go on a Strike--Pa Runs the Menagerie for a Day and Wins Their Gratitude.

I did not mean any harm when I told the Japanese jugglers that they ought to kick against having those Russian cavalrymen in the show, the fellows who ride horses standing up, in the wild-west department, 'cause I had listened to their Russian talk, and it seemed to me they were spies who were looking for a chance to do injury to the "poor little Japs." I could see that I made the Japs mad the first thing, and then I told them that pa and all the managers of the show felt sorry for the little Japs, 'cause some day the big Russians would ride right over them, and kill them right in the ring. I said that everybody thought the Japs ought to resign from the show, for fear of a clash with the Russians, or else they ought to have some grown persons to act as chaperones.

You ought to have seen the look of scorn on the faces of the Jap jugglers when the interpreter told them that the circus people were afraid the Russians would hurt them. They jabbered awhile, and then the interpreter told me that the ten little Japs could whip the 20 Russians in four minutes. Probably it was none of my business, and I never ought to have repeated it, but in a circus everybody wants to know everything that is going on, so when the big leader of the Russians asked me what those brown monkeys were talking about, I told him: "Nothing particular, only they say the ten of them could lick you 20 Russians in four minutes."

Gee, didn't that Russian talk kopec and damski, and froth at the mouth. Then he called his Russians together, and the talk sounded as though a soda fountain had burst. Then they all yelled: "Killovitch the monkey-ouskis."

I went and told pa there was going to be a riot between the Jap jugglers and the Russian horsemen, and probably the fight would take place when the Japs came out of the ring at the afternoon performance, and the Russians went in, right near the dressing-room. I asked pa not to mix in it, but keep away in the animal tent. Pa said, not much, he wouldn't be away, and he told all the managers, and they all got around the dressing-room to stop the muss, if one started.

Well, to show how the Japs were organized, as soon as they felt there was going to be a row, they kept their eyes on the Russians all the time they were in the ring doing their pole balancing, and the little Jap up on the bamboo pole, with a fan, kept jabbering to the fellows down on the ground, and I could see that trouble was coming. When their act was over the Japs bowed to the audience, and started out where the Russians were lined up to come riding in. The big Russian said: "Look at the little monkeys," but he hadn't got the words out of his mouth before the Japs turned, and every man grabbed the tail of every other horse, and jumped up behind the Russians, and each of the ten Japs took a Russian by the neck with a jiu jitsu strangle hold, and reached out his leg and wound it around the Russian on the next horse, and in ten seconds they had unhorsed the 20 Russians. The whole 30 men were on the ground rolling in the sawdust, the Japs rolling over and under the Russians, twisting their legs and arms in an unknown manner, and making them yell for help like a mastiff that has trifled in an overbearing manner with a little bulldog, until the bulldog got mad and began the chewing act on the mastiff's fore leg.

It was the worst mix-up ever was and the managers told pa to put a stop to it, and pa pulled off his coat and grabbed the first Jap he could dig out, and began to pull him, like you would take hold of the leg of a dog in a fight.

Pa said: "Here, quit this foolishness, 'cause there is an armistice, and the war is over, anyway."

O! O! but the Jap didn't do a thing to pa. He grabbed pa by the wrist, and he seemed to be having an epileptic fit, and pa's leg shot out so his feet hit a guy pole, and then the Jap pulled him back like he was a rubber ball on a string, and then he took pa by the elbow and held him out at arm's length, and then swung him around a few times and let go of him, and he fell down among the reserved seats which representatives of the press occupy. Pa stood on one ear on a crushed chair, with his legs over the railing, and when he came to, the newspaper men wanted to interview pa. Pa said all he remembered was that the air ship was sailing over the town, and they threw him out for ballast, and he struck a church spire and bounded onto a warehouse filled with dynamite, which exploded when he struck it, and the neighbors picked his remains up on a dustpan and emptied them in here, Then he asked if his head was on straight, and the circusmen took him away to the hospital tent.

The circus hands separated the Russians and Japs, or at least pulled off the Japs, and the Russians limped to the dressing-room, and their act was cut out. Unless the terms of peace between Japan and Russia include the belligerents in our show, there will be rows every day.

Pa came to the car on crutches that night just before the train pulled out for Philadelphia, and wanted to know where I was during the fight. He said he rushed right in and grabbed a Jap in one hand and a Russian in the other, and bumped their heads together, and threw one of them towards the ring, and the other up among the seats, and he wanted to know if I thought he killed either or both of them.

I hate a boy that will deceive his father, but I told him there was talk about two performers, one a Russian and the other a Jap, that were left at the morgue, but I didn't know anything sure about it, and pa said: "I was afraid I should hurt them, but they brought it on themselves by breaking the rules of the show against fighting during a performance," and pa rolled over and groaned in his berth, and went to sleep and snored so the freaks wanted to have a nose bag, such as horses eat out of, pulled over pa's face.

The queerest thing that ever happened in the circus business in this country took place at Germantown, Pa. The teamsters went on a strike at Pittsburg, for increase in wages and shorter hours, and for two days the management had a great time.

We had to get drays to haul the stuff from the train to the lot, and then our teamsters got the local draymen to join them, and when we got ready to haul the stuff back to the train nobody would do any work, and the walking delegates from the Teamsters' union just took possession of the show, and we were stuck, like an automobile when the gasoline gives out.

We had got to looking at the teamsters as of no particular account when they walked out, but when they wouldn't work, they became the most important part of the show, and after the show was over the managers who had told the striking teamsters to go plumb, found that they had gone plumb, and they had to rush all over Pittsburg and find them, and grant their demands, and get them to go to work.

Pa was sent out to find a bunch of them, and it cost pa over $30 to get them out of a beer garden, and back to the lot, and it was almost daylight before we got our train started for the next town.

Well, at the next town we could see there was something the matter with the animals. They acted as though they had lost all interest in the success of the show, and wouldn't do any of their stunts worth a cent. The elephants went through their act carelessly, and when they were scolded or prodded with the iron hook, they got mad and wanted to fight, and when they got back from the ring to the animal tent they wouldn't eat the baled hay but threw it all over the tent, and acted riotous.

The kangaroos would not do their boxing act, the horses kicked at their hay, and wouldn't eat their oats, the camels growled at their food, and scared the people who passed by where they were tied to stakes, the sacred cattle got their backs up and acted as though they, being pious, couldn't swear, but would like to hire the hyenas to swear for them; the giraffes laid down and curled their necks so they were no attraction to the show, 'cause a giraffe is no curiosity unless he stretches himself away up towards the top of the tent. The zebras rolled in the mud and spoiled their stripes, so people couldn't tell them from common mules; the grizzly bear walked his cage, and kept giving vent to bear language, and the big lion was howling all the time.

The show was a failure at that town, and when we loaded the train the managers held a meeting in our car to decide what in thunder was the matter with the animals. All kinds of theories were advanced, such as poison, malaria from Indiana, and pure cussedness. After they had discussed the matter awhile, pa came in, and they asked him what he thought about it, and that tickled pa, 'cause as foolish as he looks, he helps the show out of lots of bad holes. Pa lit a cigar and put it in one side of his mouth, put his hat up on one side of his head, like he was tough, and looked wise, and said:

"Fellow fakirs, I have been watching the animals all day, and while I do not say they understand enough of the ways of human beings to be posted on labor unions, and all that, I want to tell you they are on a strike, and that grizzly and that lion are the walking delegates that are stirring them up to mischief. They may not know anything about the teamsters' strike, but they know something has happened, and they are displeased at something, and they have lost respect for the employer. They are on a strike, and the very devil is going to pay to-morrow, unless the cause of the dissatisfaction is discovered, mutual concessions made, and arbitration resorted to.

"Gentlemen, you hear me," said pa, and he sat down on the edge of the arm of the car seat.

They gave pa the laugh, but finally told him to take charge of the strike and settle it quick, but they wanted to know what he thought animals would be dissatis-fied about, as long as they got food enough to eat.

Pa said: "I'll tell you. You feed the horses and other hay-eating animals on musty baled hay, bought from contractors that may have had it on hand for five years. How would you like it if you were served with breakfast food that had been stored in a warehouse until it was mildewed? A horse or an elephant has feelings. Give them baled hay, and when they are trying to pick out a mouthful that is not spoiled, you drive along with a load of nice new-mown timothy or alfalfa, and see them make a rush for that load of hay, the way my ten-horse team did the other day for that load of cornstalks. Then the sacred cattle are hot under the collar because of the fellows who use profanity. Can you imagine a sacred cow trying to be good, and set a pious example to the heathen animals, being patient when they have to listen to swearing? You buy meat that is tainted for the lions, who like fresh meat, and the jackal, that only loves bad meat, gets the only sirloin in the lot. Let me run the menagerie to-morrow, and I will have Mr. Lion, the walking delegate, declare this strike off."

Well, they told pa to arbitrate the strike, and the next day he had a couple of loads of timothy hay, such as mother used to make, driven in and unloaded, and the horses, elephants, camels, and things almost set up a cheer for pa. The meat-eating animals were given a picnic of the freshest beef, with a little so decayed that it was only fit to be buried, for the hyenas and jackals, and every animal was happy. They did their turns better than ever, and the sacred cattle almost acted devilish.

Now the animals have declared the strike off, and they want to lick pa's hand. The owners of the show appreciate genius, and they have raised pa's salary and given him full charge of the menagerie.

CHAPTER XIII.

The Circus Strikes the Quaker City--They Go on a Ginger Ale Jag--Pa
Breaks Up an Indian War Dance and Comes Near Being Burned Alive--The
World's Fair Cannibals Have a Roast Dog Feast.

Ever since we knew the show was billed for Philadelphia for a Saturday
and that we should have to stay over Sunday in that town, there has been
symptoms of a revolt. Everybody connected with the show has a horror of
being found dead in Philadelphia. They claim it is too dead for live people,
and not very satisfactory to dead people.

A performer who was with the show last year says that nobody but the newspaper people who had free tickets attended the performances, and some of them wouldn't go in the tent unless the press agent promised to set up a free lunch, with devilish ginger ale to drink, and that the press people got riotous on ginger ale. A ginger ale jag is terrible. When a man is full of ginger ale his intestines loop the loop, and tie up in knots, and gripe like cholera infantum, and unless his friends hold him he goes out into the world and wants to kill the women and children, and non-combatants.

Last year our press agents filled up the members of the local press with ginger ale, and when we struck Philadelphia this time the newspapers had sworn out warrants for our show, on the charge of compounding a felony, which I suppose is the legal name for ginger ale. The way the Quakers patronize a show is to put on their gray clothes, and their big white hats and stand on the corners when the parade goes by, and never crack a smile, or act interested, and when the parade has passed they go to the circus lot and see the balloon ascension, and stand on wagon wheels and try to look over the side of the tent at the performance, and then they kick because the audience on the back seats cut off their view from the wagon wheels.

Last year our show killed a Quaker, and the community is down on us. The Quaker got in the show because he owned a half inch of ground that its tents were on, and he stood right by the ring, and when the champion female rider was suspended in the air between two bareback horses, he leaned over too far inside the ring, and she kicked his hat clear up to the roof of the tent, and a female trapeze performer up there caught it and sat down on it on the trapeze. The old Quaker had heart disease and fell dead. What the Quakers complained of was that after the Quaker's remains had been removed from the ring, that the show went right on. They claimed that we ought to have shown proper respect for the dead by closing the show for 30 days, and wearing crape on our arms, but a circus is not built that way.

Ordinarily it may be quiet enough in Philadelphia on Sunday, but pa found that he had more of a run for his money than at any place we have been so far. We have had a tribe of Indians with our wild west department all summer, and pa has not stood very well with the Indians since he was in charge of the show at Fort Wayne, and they all got drunk, and he had them tied up to the poles around the ring until they got sober. They have laid for pa ever since, and it was only a matter of time when they got him. Then at Pittsburg our manager picked up a company of cannibals that had got left over from the St. Louis fair, and who agreed to perform for their board and clothes, and as they don't wear any clothes to speak of, and only eat dog week days, and hope to get a human being to roast on Sunday, it seemed a pretty good bargain.

Well, the Indians got permission to hold a green corn dance in a piece of woods near the circus lot, and the management got them a wagon load of corn, and they had built a fire and were roasting the corn, and dancing, and pa didn't know about it, and just after dark the Quaker who owned the woods complained to pa, who was on watch Sunday night, that his Indians had got off the reservation and were preparing to go on the warpath, and he wanted them to get off his premises. Pa said he would go right over and drive them back to the tents.

I tried to get pa to let the police go and drive them off, but he said he hadn't no time to go and wake up the police, and they wouldn't get around anyway before the middle of the week. So pa took a tent stake and started for the green corn roast. The

Indians were taking turns dancing and eating roasted corn, and they had a barrel of beer, and I knew enough about Indians to keep away from them when they mix beer with green corn, for it has about the same effect as committing suicide with carbolic acid.

Pa put his hat on one side of his head and went right into the midst of the Indians, and grabbed a chief called "One Ear at a Time," and hit him with the tent stake, and knocked him down, and said, "Now, you git." Well, sir, that Indian had no more than struck the fire in a sitting position, and filled the air with the odor of fried buckskin, before the whole tribe jumped on pa, and they kicked him with their moccasins, and were going to murder him, while the chief who acted as the burnt offering got out of the fire, and sat down in the cold mud to cool himself. He held up his hand as a signal of attention, and he called a council of war, while the squaws sat on pa to hold him down.

The council of war sentenced pa to be burned at the stake, and they tied him to a tree and began to pile sticks around him, and pa told me to go to the circus lot and give an alarm, and send the hands to rescue him. Gee, but didn't I run though, and yell an alarm big enough for a massacre. I told the hands, who were sleeping under the seats, or playing cards on the trunks that the Indians were burning pa at the stake, and some of the hands said that would serve him right, and the fellows that were playing cards said they didn't want to break up the game when they were losers, to rescue no baldheaded curmudgeon. I thought pa was a goner, sure, 'cause I could hear the Indians yell, and I thought I could smell flesh burning. Oh, but I was scared for fear they would burn pa alive.

Just then the man who had charge of our cannibals, who each had a dog that they were looking for a place to roast, came along and I told him about the Indians' corn roast, and he ordered the cannibals to go drive the Indians away from their fire and roast their dogs. Well, it worked like a charm, and the cannibals made a rush for the Indians and drove them away just as they had lighted the fire around pa, and we were not a minute too soon. After the Indians had skedaddled for the woods, and we cut the cords that bound pa, the cannibals went to work and skun the dogs, and began to cook them, and pa looked on, until it made him squirmish, but he was so tickled at being saved from the Indians, that he tried to be a good fellow with the cannibals. I guess it would have been all right, only the cannibals got to drinking the Philadelphia beer, and then it was all off, cause roast dog wasn't good enough for them, and they wanted to roast pa.

First they offered pa dog to eat, but he had swore off on dog, and passed on it, and that made the cannibals mad, and they got ready to roast pa, and I guess they would have eaten him half cooked, if it hadn't been for the performers and freaks who had missed their pet dogs, and the circus hands told them the cannibals had just gone to the woods with a mess of dogs to roast for a dog feast.

Well, they were just getting a fire around pa, and he was giving the grand hailing sign of distress, when the performers, headed by the fat woman, whose peeled Mexican dog was lost in the shuffle, came in amongst the cannibals, and pa and the other dogs were rescued, in the darnedest fight I ever saw. The performers just walked right over the cannibals, and mauled them with stakes, and all the dogs that had not been killed were pulled away from the heathen, and saved. The fat woman got her dog all right, and when pa came up from the stake where they were going to burn him, and congratulated her on recovering her dog, she turned on pa and accused him of being the leading cannibal, and that he was the one who put up the whole job to steal the dogs. She jabbed him with a parasol, but pa was innocent.

The Indians got back to the tent along towards morning, and the cannibals went back with us, and we had to feed them on wieners, which was the nearest to roast dog we could get for them at that time of night.

Pa seems to get it in the neck in this show, 'cause everything that goes wrong is laid to him, and if anything goes right, somebody else gets the credit, and I think he would resign if it was not for his pride. After the trouble about the Indians and the cannibals the manager called pa up and reprimanded him for indulging the tribes in their wild orgies, and said he couldn't maintain discipline as long as pa mixed up with them and encouraged them in such things.

Pa tried to explain that he was the victim instead of being the cause of the dog roast, but the manager dismissed pa by telling him not to let it occur again. Then to show the inconsistency of the manager, he ordered pa to go on ahead of the show to New York, and advertise that the cannibals in our show would give an exhibition of roasting and eating a human being, and to offer a reward for anybody that would consent to be roasted and eaten in public.

Pa has gone to New York to look for somebody who will take the position of meat for the cannibals, and he is instructed to spare no expense to find such a man. He thinks he may find somebody connected with the Life Insurance scandal, who has lost all desire to live any longer, and who will gladly go into this "mutual" scheme. I don't know.

This circus business is too much for me, 'cause I am losing friends all the time. Even the monkeys have got so they seem to be ashamed to be seen talking to me, and when I pass the monkey cage they turn their backs on me, as though I did not belong to their set. When a fellow gets so low that monkeys feel above him, and throw out sarcastic remarks when he goes by, it is time to change your luck some way.

CHAPTER XIV.

A Newport Monk Is Added to the Show--The Boy Teaches Him Some "Manly Tricks"--The Tent Blows Down and a Panic Follows--Pa Manages the Animal Act Which Ends in a Novel Manner.

We have added to the show the most remarkable animal that ever was--a baboon that dresses like a man, and eats at a table, using a knife and fork, and a napkin. This baboon has been playing an engagement with the Four Hundred at Newport, dining with the crowned heads at that resort, but the confounded baboon got to be too human, and he fell in love with an heiress, and scared one of the Willie boys that was also in love with her. His friends were afraid that the baboon would cut Willie out entirely, or get jealous and injure Willie, so the manager of the Four Hundred show decided to banish the baboon, and our show sent pa to Newport to buy the baboon and bring him to our show at New York.

We had the darndest time getting him away from Newport. Pa couldn't do any with him, but he took to me, 'cause he thought I was his long-lost brother, and I could do anything with him. We got him in our stateroom on the boat, and took his clothes away from him, 'cause he only wears his clothes when he is being dined and wined, and we chained him in the upper berth. He just raised the very deuce on the way down to New York. After pa and I got to sleep that baboon got my clothes, and put them on, slipped the chain over his head, jumped through the transom, and went into every berth where the transom was open, and chatted with the people who occupied the berths. There was an old man and woman from New Hampshire in one berth, and when the monk got in their berth and began to talk the Newport language, the old man thought it was me, and he said: "Now, bub, you go away to your pa."

The monk went out, and got into another berth, and crawled under the bunk, and when the woman came in to go to bed, she looked under it to see if any man was there. When she saw our baboon she yelled "fire," and the officers of the boat pulled him out by the hind leg, and tore my pant leg off. Pa and I had to sit up the rest of the night with him, and when we landed him with the show at Madison Square Garden we felt relieved.

One woman on the boat has followed us ever since to collect damages from pa, 'cause his oldest son, the monk, proposed to her. Gee, it seems to me a woman ought to know the difference between a baboon and a man, but some women will marry anything that wears clothes.

The monk took to me so, Pa said I must teach him everything I could that men do, so I thought it would do no harm to teach him to chew tobacco, 'cause he could already smoke cigarettes, so I borrowed a chew from the boss canvasman, a great big chew of black plug tobacco, and the monk grabbed it, and chewed it awhile, just before the afternoon performance, and swallowed it. I knew that settled the monk, and when the audience came along by his cage, and pa was trying to get him to perform, as he did at Newport, eating dinner like a man, the monk turned pale, and his stomach ached, and he stood on his head, and held his stomach in both hands, and kicked the table over. Then he hit pa a swat with his foot, and wound his tail around pa's neck, and laid his head on pa's shirt bosom, and was seasick.

Pa said: "Well, this beats everything. What did you do to him?"

I told pa I had only been teaching the monk manly tricks, and pa said: "Well, you have overdone it." And then the Humane society had pa arrested for cruelty to animals. But the monk got over it, and now he tries to be a masher, and winks at women, and flirts with them just as the men do at Newport.

*　　　*　　　*　　　*　　　*

We thought we were smart when we held up the railroad for damages back in Pennsylvania, after the wreck, but we are getting a dose of our own medicine. At Poughkeepsie there came up a wind and rainstorm that blew the tent down right in the midst of the evening performance, and scared everybody half to death. Several people were hit by tent poles and hurt some, and it was the wildest scene I ever saw, and people who got out alive ran away in the dark, and somebody said the animals had all got loose, and some of the people never stopped running till daylight the next morning.

Some run into the river, and the ambulances carried the injured to hospitals. Pa stampeded with the elephants, and never showed up till noon the next day. By that time at least 1,000 people had filed claims for damages, and all the lawyers from Albany to New York were on our trail.

The managers appointed pa to settle with the injured, and the way he argued with those people was a caution. One old woman was killed, and pa tried to show her relatives that as she was old and helpless, and more or less a burden to the family, they ought to pay the show something for getting her off their hands. One tramp had his feet cut off, and pa tried to show him how much he would save in shoes the rest of his life, and that he was in big luck. We left pa at Poughkeepsie to settle the cases, and went on to New York, and we heard the people had lynched him, but he showed up in a couple of days with money left. Now all the lawyers in New York are after us with claims and they have attached most everything, and the show is up against it.

What a difference it makes who wants damages. When we were working the railroad for damages, it was a cinch, and like getting money from home, but now that the people are working us for damages, for being smashed up under our tent, we look upon it as a crime, and tell them it is an act of Providence, and that the show is not to blame for a windstorm. But the lawyers can't be very pious, for they won't believe in the act of Providence racket, and we shall have to cough up all the profits of the season.

Since we got settled in New York for a two weeks' stand, in Madison Square Garden, we are having the tents repaired, and don't have to put up and take down tents, and ride all night on trains. We are all stopping at hotels and getting rested, and pa is having a chance to shine.

The managers think pa is trying to commit suicide, for he wants to take the place of anybody who is sick or drunk, and is the understudy of everybody. We got one act that just curdles your blood, a cage in the ring, with lions and tigers and leopards, who go through all kinds of stunts. One lion rides a horse and jumps through hoops, and lands on the back of the horse, and jumps on a staging and lets the horse go around the ring, and then jumps on again. The horse is blindfolded, so he don't know it is a lion that jumps on his back, but thinks it is a man.

The tigers ride bicycles, and the leopards jump about wherever the trainer tells them to; a monkey acts as clown, and a little elephant runs a make-believe automobile. That act alone is worth the price of admission.

Well, the regular trainer went to Coney Island, and got drunk, and we either had to cut out that performance, or give back the money, and the manager was wailing about it, 'cause nothing makes a circus man wail like giving back good money. Then pa said he would save the day by taking charge of the animal act. He said he had watched it every day, and knew how to do it, and he could dress up in the clothes of the regular trainer, and the animals wouldn't know the difference. Gee, but I was scared to have pa try to run that animal show, and I think everyone in the show believed it would be pa's finish. I felt like an orphan when pa came out of the dressing-room with the trainer's clothes on, though pa's stomach was so big you would think a blindfolded horse would know pa was no trainer.

Well, pa went in the round cage made of bar iron, and motioned to the attendants to send the animals into the cage through the chute from the animal quarters. The first to come were two tigers that were to ride velocipedes. I trembled for pa when they went in and waved their tails and looked at pa as much as to say: "O, we won't do a thing to you." They actually looked at each other and winked; but pa motioned to the velocipedes, and looked fierce, and when they hesitated about getting on, pa said: "You won't, won't you," and he took a club filled with lead and started for the biggest tiger. He hesitated a moment, and then he jumped on the machine, and the other followed, and they raced around, and then pa made them get off and jump hurdles. Finally he motioned to a shelf for them to jump up onto, and when they hesitated he kicked one in the slats, and hit the other with the club, and they went up on that shelf too quick, but they stayed there and snarled at pa, and I was afraid they would jump on him when his back was turned.

Then they brought in the blind horse and the lion, and the lion was onto pa, and he struck right off. He got up on the pedestal from which he was to jump onto the horse's back, but when the horse came around the lion wouldn't jump, and pa said: "I'll give you one more chance," and the horse went under the lion, and he wouldn't jump. So pa stopped the horse and took an iron bar and knocked the lion off onto the floor, and he growled at pa, but pa kept mauling him, and finally the lion jumped up on the pedestal and seemed to say: "Bring on your horse," and pa started the horse, and Mr. Lion made his jumps all right, and the audience cheered pa.

All the animals went through their stunts all right, but I thought I could see they were laying for pa, and I wished he was out of the cage. The wind-up came when the lions were seated on benches, and the elephant was between them, and the tigers and leopards made a pyramid, and the monkey was clawing around pa's legs. The signal was about to be given for the animals to return through the chute, when the monkey tackled pa's legs like a football player, the elephant pushed pa over, and the lions pawed him and snarled, and the tigers took a mouthful out of pa's pants, and the leopards snatched his red coat off, and the signal was given for them to get out of the cage, and they went out like boys at recess, leaving pa in the cage with the blind horse, with not clothes enough left on him to wad a gun. He was not even scratched, however, the animals having just combined to humiliate pa.

The audience cheered. Pa said "Well, wouldn't that skin you." They threw him an overcoat to put on, and he bowed like a hero, and quit the ring cage, and was met outside by the whole show management, and congratulated on having more nerve than any man alive.

Pa said: "If you will give me a shotgun loaded with bird shot, I will make those animals get on their knees at the next performance, and beg my pardon. You can discharge your trainer, and I will teach them a lot of new stunts."

Say, pa is a wonder, and he has already got old Barnum beat a block.

CHAPTER XV.

The Bad Boy Feeds the Menagerie Scotch Snuff--Pa Gets Mauled by the Sneezing Animals--Pa Takes a Midnight Ride on a Mule to Escape Punishment.

Well, I s'pose I have done it now and it would not surprise me to be killed and fed to wild animals,' The manager of the show was talking to pa and me, before we left New York, about the condition of the show. Its finances were all balled up on account of settling with people who pretended to be injured when the tent blew down at Poughkeepsie, and the hands and performers are kicking because we are a month behind on salaries, and they get drunk whenever any jay will buy for them. Everybody gives passes to everybody that wants to get in the show, so the box office man has a sinecure, and people chase us from town to town for money for board, and hay and everything.

All through New Jersey we showed to claim agents and creditors, and didn't take in money enough to buy meat for the animals. He said the animals had all taken cold, and lay around dormant, and didn't take any interest in the business, and the manager told pa he must think of something to wake the animals up. Pa said he would leave it to me to wake 'em up, and get some ginger into them. I told pa if I had five dollars to spend I could make every animal jump like a box car. Pa gave me the money, and I went and bought five pounds of Scotchsnuff, and divided it up into ounce packages, and started during the afternoon performance at Wilmington, Del., to wake up the animals.

There is something peculiar about animals, if you try to give them anything that they think you want them to take, you can't drive it down them with a pile driver, but if you try to hide something where they can reach it, they watch you out of one eye, and when you go away they look at you as much as to say: "O, you think you are smart, don't you?" Then they will go and dig it up, and play with it, and eat it if they want to.

I took my first package of snuff to the lion's cage, and he was the sickest and most disgusted looking lion you ever saw, acting like a man who has taken a severe cold, and wants to kill anybody that looks at him. The lion lay on the straw, stretched out full length, paying no attention to the crowd that passed his cage, and acting as though he wanted a hot whisky and his feet soaked in mustard water. When he was not looking I hid the package of snuff under the straw, and rattled the straw a little, and he opened his eyes and looked at me as much as to say: "You can't fool old Shadrack, for I am onto you." I walked away behind the hyena cage, and Mr. Lion got up and stretched himself, and walked to the place where I put the paper of snuff, put his foot on it and broke the paper, and then he put his nose down and sniffed a sniff that drew the whole of the snuff up into his nose and lungs, and insides generally.

Gee, but you never saw such a change in a lion. The crowd of visitors were right near his cage, when he sniffed, and when he got the snuff into him, he began to heave his sides like a man who is preparing to sneeze, caught his breath a few times, and let out a sneeze that sounded like the explosion of an automobile tire. It threw cut feed all over the audience, and everybody ran away yelling that the lion busted.

He kept on sneezing, and looking so astounded, as though he couldn't make out what had got into him. Pa heard the commotion and came running up to the cage to find out what ailed the lion. After I had gone around to the other cages and put snuff in all of them, I came up to the lion's cage. The lion had stopped sneezing and was roaring and jumping up and down, with his mouth open, trying to catch his breath, like a man who has taken too big a dose of fresh horse-radish.

Pa said: "What have you been doing to Shadrack?"

I told pa I had woke Shadrack up, and that in about a minute he would find that the whole animal kingdom had got a bellyful, and would join in the chorus.

Pa tried to soothe the lion by going up to the cage and stroking his mane, but the lion looked cross-eyed and stopped prancing and gave a sneeze right at pa, which blew pa clear across the tent to where the sacred cow had just got hers. When the stuff began to work on that cow it was simply scandalous, 'cause she bellowed and cried and sneezed all at once, and pawed pa. He got up and told me I was overdoing this waking up act on the animals.

By that time the cage of hyenas began to sneeze a quartette, and fight each other, and the atmosphere about their cage was full of hair and language that would be much like cussing if it could be translated into English. Pa tried to quiet the crowd and silence the hyenas by taking an iron bar and mauling them, but the hyenas just backed up against the rear of the cage and howled and sneezed at pa, and dared him to come on.

One of them caught him by the shirt sleeve and tore pa's shirt off and eat it. Pa was a sight, with no shirt on, and he ought to have gone to the dressing room and slicked, but just then the camels and the giraffes, who had inhaled their snuff, began to sneeze and beg to be killed, and pa had to go over there and quiet them. A camel is the solemnist looking beast on earth when he tries to be good natured, but when he is sick and mad, and full of snuff, he is a fiend. One such camel is enough for a man to handle, but when 14 camels are all sneezing at once, and trying to locate the person that is responsible for their trouble, it is the safest to keep away, and when pa went in amongst them, with no shirt on, and the Arab keepers had run away in fright, it was a dangerous thing to do.

But pa is brave even to rashness. He went up to Mahomet, the double-humped leader of the herd, who was the leader of the sneezers, and kicked him in the slats and told him to hush up his noise. He clubbed him on the humps with a tent stake. Then there was a rebellion in Egypt, and Mahomet bit pa, and wouldn't let go, and the other camels sneezed all over pa, and had him down, walking on him with their padded feet. The circus hands had to pull pa out, and it wasn't so bad, because the crowd remained and they thought it was a part of the show, and that the animals were trained to sneeze that way.

The worst case was the hippopotamus. He was so big, and had such big nostrils, that I laid about half a pound of snuff on the side of his tank, and when he snuffed it up his nose he got it all. I heard a howl from the tank and the herd, who was the leader of the sneezers, and I told pa to come on, 'cause Vessuvious was going to erupt.

Pa came on the run, just as he was, and then the worst happened. I think the hippo went under water when he found the sneeze was coming, for just as pa got to the tank the water flew into the air like a torpedo had exploded under a battle-ship, and the hippo had sneezed all right and pa and the audience which had followed him were drenched and deafened by the explosion. The hippo had blown the water all out of his tank, and he lay at the bottom, on his side, sneezing little sneezes not louder than the report of a six-pound cannon, and panting for breath. Then he raised his head, got up on his feet, and opened his mouth like a gash cut in a steer by a cow catcher of an engine, and he yawned, and I guess he got the lockjaw, 'cause he kept his mouth open all the afternoon to get the air, like a soprano singer in a choir, who has been fed a cayenne pepper lozenger by the tenor, just before she gets up to sing: "A Charge to Keep, I Have."

We went around and inspected the sneezing animals with the manager, and he complimented me by saying I had saved the show from becoming an aggregation of stuffed animals, only fit for a taxidermist studio, and made every animal show that he had ginger in him. He wanted me to try my snuff cure on the performers and freaks, 'cause they were getting to be dead ones.

Well, before the day was over at Wilmington, Del., pa was scared worse than he ever was in all his life before. The state of Delaware is the only state that punishes criminals by tying them up and whipping them on the bare back with a cat-o'-nine-tails, and all our men had been warned to be good while they were in Delaware, 'cause if they committed any crime there was no power on earth that could save them from being publicly horsewhipped. Pa himself impressed it on the men to look out that they didn't get into any trouble. Gee, but the fear of a public whipping makes men good.

Twenty years ago some hold-up men from New York robbed a bank in Delaware, and were caught, and given 50 lashes apiece on the bare back, by a big negro, and there has never been a burglary in Delaware since. We thought we would play a joke on pa, so the manager told pa that constables were looking for him to arrest him for cruelty to animals, for kicking a camel in the stomach, and hitting the camel with an iron bar, and that if pa didn't want to be publicly horsewhipped on the bare back he better skip out for Washington, D.C., where we would show in a couple of days, and wait for us.

Pa was so frightened he couldn't get supper, and everybody talked about cats of nine tails, and how prisoners were cut to pieces, and every time pa saw a jay with a slouch hat he thought it was a constable after him. After dark he put on an old suit of clothes and said he was going to Washington. They told him if he went to take a train he would surely be arrested at the depot, so pa put a saddle on one of the mules, and rode out of town and rode all night, and all the next day he bought oats of farmers to be delivered at Wilmington for the circus. Finally he got out of Delaware, and the next day the farmers came in with the oats, but the show was gone, and they won't do a thing to pa if he ever shows up in Delaware again.

Pa met us at the depot in Washington, but he was ever so changed from his long ride and anxiety over the possibility of being arrested and pilloried, and lambasted by a negro in Delaware. He said to me, with a trembling voice: "Hennery, this 'ere show business is too much for your pa. I would rather be a Mormon, in Utah, with 40 wives, and several hundred children, and long whiskers. I am a changed man, Hennery, and afraid of my shadow."

CHAPTER XVI.

A Senator's Son Bets the Bad Boy That Elephants Are Cowards--They Let a Bag of Rats Loose at the Afternoon Performance--The Elephants Stampede, Pa Fractures a Rib and General Pandemonium Reigns.

Gee, but I must be an easy mark. I have got so I bet on a sure thing, and when a fellow bets on a sure thing he is bound to lose.

It was this way. The show arrived in Washington, D. C., on a Sunday morning, and, as usual, all the boys in town came to the lot to see us put up the tents. I was around with pa and the boss canvasman, and the town boys could see I belonged to the show, and they envied me and wanted to get acquainted with me so I would let them walk around with me, and go into the tents Sunday afternoon and see the animals.

There was one boy with a sort of rough rider hat on, and buckskin fringe on his pants, and everybody said he was a senator's son, but the other boys had rather be acquainted with me, because I belonged to the show, and I took pity on the senator's son and let him talk to me, without looking cross at him, or snubbing him, as I do most boys who try to butt in on me. I got to liking the senator's son and had him come in the tent, and we put in the afternoon looking at the animals.

The elephants were chewing hay and looking fierce, and the senator's boy said elephants were the greatest cowards on earth, and I said, "Not on your life; the giant in our show is the greatest coward, and the behemoth of holy writ is next." The senator's son said elephants were such cowards they were afraid of mice, and we could take a trap full of mice and turn them loose in the ring and the elephants would stampede, and he would bet five dollars on it. I excused myself for a moment and told pa what the senator's son offered to bet, and pa said: "Here's $50, and you can take all the bets you can get. Why, this herd of elephants would walk on mice, and rats, too. You bet with him and tell him to bring along all the rats and mice he can find in the white house, and you can turn them into the ring Monday afternoon when the elephants do their turn, and if an elephant bats an eye I will eat his ears for mushrooms."

I went back to young Mr. Senator and took his bet, and told him I had plenty more money to bet the same way, and he said the next afternoon he would come with his mice and rats, and a lot of money to bet that you couldn't hold that flock of elephants with log chains when he opened his bag of rats and mice.

Well, how it got into the papers I do not know, but the next morning they all said an interesting experiment would be made the next afternoon at the great and only circus, to determine once and for all whether elephants were afraid of mice, and that a senator's son and a son of one of the proprietors of the show would conduct the experiment by turning loose a lot of mice and rats in the rings at precisely 3:30 p.m.

Well, you never saw such a crowd in a circus as we had that afternoon. It seemed as though the whole population turned out, foreign ministers, negroes, society people and clerks. That senator's son and the whole family, and the neighbors, must have been up all night catching mice and rats, and it took nine boys and three servants to carry the baskets and traps and bags of mice and rats. I passed them all in and we lined up on a front seat to wait for the elephant stunt, and when the thing was ripe we were to empty the whole mess of vermin into the ring.

I felt as though something was wrong 'cause I saw the new moon over my left shoulder the night before, and now I wish I had died before this thing happened. When the Japanese jugglers went out of the ring I knew that was the cue for the elephants to come in, and when the dressing room curtain was pulled aside and old Bolivar came out at the head of the herd, and they marched around the outside of the ring, clear around the tent, my heart jumped up into my throat, and I felt sick.

The senator's son said: "When these rats and things begin to chase your old elephants, you won't be able to see their tails for the dust they will kick up."

Then I thought of the money pa had given me to bet, and I offered to bet it all, and a negro produced funds and took all my bets like a bookmaker.

Well, after doing a turn around the big ring, the trainer steered the elephants into the middle ring, and the great audience leaned forward to catch every trick the elephants did.

Us boys held on to the bags that the mice and things were in, waiting for our cue. The elephants stood on their heads and hind feet, and fore feet, laid down, fired pistols, and did everything just right, without making a mistake. Finally the trainer formed the whole herd into a grand pyramid, with old Bolivar in the center, each elephant holding an American flag with his trunk, and waving it, and the audience broke out into a cheer that fairly ripped the canvas.

Then I said to young Mr. Senator: "Come on with your rats, now, and I win $50." All hands picked up the baskets and bags and went to the side of the ring and emptied the whole bunch of more than 500 into the ring. The rats and mice rushed for the elephants, and then turned and made a rush for the reserved seats.

Oh, dear, what a time we had. The elephants got down off that pyramid so quick it would make your head swim, and old Bolivar trumpeted in abject fear, and tried to break away, but pa came along with a tent stake and hit Bolivar over the head, and told the trainer to put the elephants back into the pyramid and hold them there till the bell rung for them to cease their stunt. The trainer couldn't do anything with them, and they bellowed and dodged mice and shied at rats, and Bolivar took his trunk and swatted pa clear across the ring.

The elephants followed Bolivar to the main entrance, each elephant trying to walk on the heels of the one ahead of him, and all the circus hands trying to head off the elephants, but they wouldn't head off. They were simply scared to death, and they broke out the side of the tent near the lemonade stand and went whooping out into the open air and freedom, while the audience yelled with joy.

Young Mr. Senator said to me: "What do you think of elephants now?"

I told him to take his money and he darned.

The audience was getting nervous, so the band struck up "A Hot Time in the Old Town," and they were quieting down as the curtain raised and the horses for the chariot race came out. Just then a woman with red socks got up on her chair in the press seats and pulled her dress away up and yelled, "Rats!" and another woman screamed and jumped up on a seat with her clothes at half mast, and yelled that there were mice on the seats. In less than two minutes every woman in the audience, and the bearded woman, and the fat woman, were standing up on something, holding up their dresses and shaking their skirts and screaming, and when the fat woman fell into the arms of the bearded woman, in a faint, and the bearded woman dropped the fat woman, pa told the bearded woman he was ashamed of her screaming, 'cause she ought to be more of a man than that.

Well, every mouse and rat in the bunch seemed to be looking for women to scream at them, and there was no use trying to run a show with such an excited audience, so pa had the band play "Good Night, Ladies," and he announced that the performance might be considered over for the afternoon. Everybody made a rush for the exits. Each woman held up her skirts and fairly galloped to get away from the mice and rats.

They all got out of the tent finally, and then the managers had a meeting to find out who started the trouble, and what it was best to do about it. I was sitting alone on a front seat, thinking over the scenes of the afternoon, and wondering what the young senator's son would do with the money he had won of me, and whether he had depopulated the white house of rats and mice, so the president would notice it. I was thinking about elephants and wondering if they were cowards by nature, or had acquired cowardice by associating with mankind, when pa came along and sat down by me, a picture of despair, 'cause Bolivar had fractured one of his ribs, and the fat woman had paralyzed his knees sitting on his lap while they brought her to after she fainted when she thought a rat was climbing into her sock.

Pa sighed, and said: "Hennery, I wanted an exciting life, to keep me from brooding over advancing age, and I chose the circus business, but I find it is rather too strenuous for me. Each day something occurs to try my nerves. I do not claim that you are to blame for it all, but I think I could enjoy my position with the show if you would take the first train that goes north, and leave me for awhile. What I need is rest. Go, boy, go!"

I felt sorry far pa, but I put my arm around him, and I said: "Pa, do not fear. I will never desert you, until the season is over. Wherever you go, I will go, and I will keep you awake, don't fear. Now that we are going into the sunny south, where every man may have it in for you, 'cause you were a Yankee soldier, I will stay by you, and there will be things doing that will make you think the past has been a sweet dream. See, pa!"

Pa sighed again, and said: "This is too much!" and he rushed off to find the elephants.

CHAPTER XVII.

The Bad Boy and the Senator's Son Go on an Elephant Chase--The
Senator's Son Gets His Friend a Bid to Dinner at the White
House--The Trained Seal Swallows an Alarm Clock.

The show remained in Washington two days, 'cause it took all one day and night to catch the elephants, after the senator's boy and I turned the rats and mice loose in the ring while the elephants were forming a pyramid. Pa and all the circus hands had to go away down towards the Bull Run battlefield to round them up, and young Mr. Senator let me ride one of his ponies and he and I went along to help catch the elephants.

We went out through Alexandria towards Bull Run battlefield. There we overtook pa and the boss canvasman and the elephant handler, and we met some farmers coming into Alexandria with their families, stampeding like people out west when the Indians go on the warpath. They had got up in the morning to milk the cows and found about 20 elephants in the barnyard, making the cows do a song and dance. Pa told them there was no danger at all, 'cause he would take any elephant by the tail and snap its head off, like boys snap the heads off garter snakes, and I told them that me and the senator's boy stampeded the elephants and we could drive them back to town like a drove of sheep.

The farmers thought we were great and they followed us back to the farm, where we found the herd of elephants had taken possession and were having the time of their lives. About a dozen of the big elephants had found a couple of barrels of cider in a shed and had been drinking it, and when we got there they were like section hands with jags on.

Bolivar, the big elephant, was the drunkest, and when he saw pa coming with the gang of hands, with ropes and spears, he winked at the other elephants and seemed to say: "Watch me tree 'em," for he came out of the gate and bellowed, and made a charge at the gang, and pa beat them all going up crab apple trees. The senator's son saw pa up a tree, and he said: "Old gentleman, if these are your animals, or insects, or whatever they are, you ought to come down off your perch and take them to a Keeley cure, because they are intoxicated."

And pa came down and took a fence rail and sharpened it with an ax, and he run it into Bolivar about a foot, and Bolivar trumpeted for surrender, and that settled the elephant strike, for pa ordered Bolivar into the road, and in five minutes the whole herd of elephants was following Bolivar back to Washington, as meek as a drunken husband being led home by his wife.

Gee, what do you think? The president heard how the senator's boy and I stampeded the elephants and invited the senator's boy to bring his young friend around to the white house to supper. Well, we went.

I forgot what we had to eat, I was so interested in the president's conversation. He talked about the show business as though he had been a ringmaster in a circus. He said he was in the show the day before when we stampeded the elephants, and he told us about his hunting trips in the west, until I could smell bacon cooking at the camp fire, and I could smell the balsam boughs they slept on, on the ground.

When he let up a little on his talk, I braced up and asked him if he had rather shoot wild cats and bears than be president. He hedged and said both occupations worked pretty well together and he had enjoyed 'em both. Then I asked him if he was going to run for president again, and he winked at his wife, and then he asked me what made me ask the question. I told him pa wanted me to find out. I told him all the boys wanted him to run, 'cause he was a good feller, and not afraid of the cars.

The president laughed and said: "Well, it's this way. The president business is a good deal like bear hunting. You get on a fresh track, either in politics or bear hunting, and follow the game with dogs, or politicians, as the case may be. The trail keeps getting fresher and by and by the game is in sight, and the dogs are nipping its hind legs, if it is a bear, or chewing big words if it is an opposing candidate, and nipping him in exposed places. You ride like mad, your clothes or your reputation torn by briars if it is a bear, or by opposition newspapers if it is a political campaign, and you wish it was over, many times, and are so tired you wish you were dead. Finally your bear or your opponent in politics is treed and the dogs are trying to climb the tree, and your bear or your political opponent is up on a limb snarling and showing his teeth at the dogs or the politicians, and then you ride up, look the ground over, wait till your heart stops beating and fire the shot at a vital part, and your bear or your political opponent comes tumbling to the ground. When he ceases to kick you put your foot on his neck and feel sorry you killed him, but you go to work and skin him and hang his hide on the fence. Then you have got to ride all night to get to camp, if it is a bear, and work harder than a man on a treadmill for four years, if it is a presidential candidate you have skun."

I had sat with my mouth open while the president talked, and never said a word, but when he quit I said: "Yes, but suppose when you got your bear skun, another bear should come after you and dare you to knock a chip off his shoulder, and growl, and walk sideways with his bristles all up, would you run, or would you stand your ground?"

"We better change the subject," said the president, and rose from the table, and we all got up. He patted me on the head, and said: "Tell your pa I will see him later, and in the meantime, you run your circus and I will try to run mine."

The queerest thing happened that night. The senator's boy spoke of our trained seals, that catch a fish if you throw it to them and swallow it whole. He said it would be fun to take a little alarm clock and sew it up in a fish, and set the alarm at seven o'clock p. m., when the crowd is watching the seals swallow fish, and throw it to the big seal, and the alarm would go off inside him.

Well, I bit like a bass, and said we would do it, so he took a little alarm clock and set it for seven o'clock. We got it into a fish, and I am ashamed to tell what happened. Gee, but that seal grabbed the fish with a clock in it, and tried to swallow it, but the brass ring caught on one of his teeth, and he was trying to get it loose when the alarm went off, and the seal jumped out of the tank and began to prance around the crowd, scaring the women, and making all the animals nervous. He stood on his head and bellowed, and all the circus hands came rushing up. Finally the alarm clock quit jingling, and they caught the seal and pulled the clock off his tooth, and just then pa came up to me and said: "What deviltry you boys up to now? Suppose that seal had swallowed that clock, and you couldn't wind it up; it might kill him. Now, go to the car, 'cause we are going to get out of this town right off. You make me tired." And pa helped to lift the slippery seal into the tank, and looked mad at his little boy, and hurt the feelings of the senator's boy.

CHAPTER XVIII.

The Show Strikes Virginia and the Educated Ourang Outang Has the Whooping Cough--The Bad Boy Plays the Part of a Monkey, but They Forget to Pin on a Tail.

Well, I have broke the show all to pieces, just by not being able to stand grief. Everything is all balled up, the managers are sore at me, and afraid of being sent to jail, and pa thinks I ought to be mauled. It was this way: When we left Washington we cut loose from every home tie, and plunged into Virginia, and the trouble began at once. We met a lawyer on the train, on the way to Richmond, and fed him in our dining car, and got him acquainted with all the performers and freaks, and he told us that we would have to be careful in Virginia, 'cause all the white people were first families and aristocratic, and if any man about our show should fail to be polite to the white people they would be shot or lynched, but if we wanted to shoot niggers the game laws were not very strict about it, 'cause the open season on niggers run the year around, but you couldn't shoot white people only two months in the year. He said another thing that scared pa and the managers. He said that if a traveling show did not perform all it advertised the owners were liable to go to state prison for 20 years, and that each town had men on the lookout to see that shows didn't advertise what they didn't carry out.

Pa and the managers held a consultation, and couldn't find that we advertised anything that we didn't have, except the ourang outang that we took on at New York, which eats and dresses like a man, 'cause that animal got whooping cough in Delaware and had to be sent to a hospital, but we heard he was well again and would join the show in a week. Pa asked the Richmond lawyer how it would be if one of the animals that was advertised was sick and couldn't perform, and he told pa the people would mob the show if anything was left out.

When we got to Richmond the whole population, principally niggers, was at the lot when we put up the tents, and everybody wanted to catch a sight of Dennis, the ourang outang, and the posters all over town that pictured Dennis smoking cigarettes with a dress suit on, and eating with a knife and fork and a napkin tucked under his chin, were surrounded by crowds. It was plain that all the people cared for was to see the monk.

The managers held a council of war and decided the show would be ruined if we didn't make a bluff at having an ourang outang, so it was decided that I was to be dressed up in Dennis' clothes, and put on a monkey mask, and go through his stunt at the afternoon performance.

Gee, but I hated to do it, but pa said the fate of the show depended on it and if I didn't take the part he would have to do it himself, and I knew pa wasn't the build of man to play the monkey, and so I said I would do it, but I will never do it again for any show. The wardrobe woman fixed my up like Dennis, and I had seen him go through his stunt so often I thought I could imitate him, and of course there was no talking to do, but just to grunt once in awhile, the way Dennis did, and have an animal look.

Well, sir, the keeper who trained the ourang outang took me in hand, and in an hour I was perfect, I had rubber feet and wore black gloves, and had a tail fastened with a safety pin, that would deceive the oldest showman in the business. When the crowd was the biggest, in the middle ring, the keeper led me out of the dressing room with a chain. The announcement was made by the barker that Dennis, the educated ourang outang, that had performed before crowned heads in Europe and sapheads in Newport, the only man-monkey in the known world, would now entertain the most select audience that had ever been under the tent. Then I was dragged into the ring and put on the platform.

They didn't put on my dress clothes at first, but had a little screen on the platform for me to go behind to dress, and I appeared first in the natural state of the ourang outang, with a suit of buffalo robe stuff that looked exactly like a big monkey. I bowed and the audience cheered, and I stood on my hands and scratched at an imaginary flea, and pa, who was leaning against the platform, whispered to me that I was making the hit of the season.

Then the attendants set the table and the keeper took me behind the screen and dressed me, and the old fool forgot to put on my tail. He led me out and I sat up to the table, hitched up my cuffs, put a napkin under my chin, took a knife and fork and began to eat, just like a human being. The audience cheered, and the circus people crowded around and said I was just as good as Dennis himself. I went through the whole of Dennis' performance and never skipped a note, until a smart white man yelled: "Where is the tail of your ourang outang?" and the crowd began to be suspicious, and more than a thousand yelled. "There is no tail on your monkey."

That rattled the trainer and he remembered that he had forgotten to pin the tail on me, so while I was using the finger bowl he went to the screen and got the tail and came out and was pinning it on to my dress pants, when the audience began to yell: "Fraud! Fraud! Kill the monk!" and a lot of stuff.

Then pa got on a barrel the elephants had been performing on and got the attention of the audience and told them not to be unreasonable. He said the management had found by experience that after the ourang outang had been trained to eat like a man and wear men's clothes, that his tail was in the way, so at a great expense the management had caused Dennis' tail to be amputated at a New York hospital, and while we always carry the tail along, it was only used when a critical audience demanded it, but if this refined audience so desired the tail would be attached to the intelligent animal.

The crowd yelled: "Pin on the tail; the tail goes with the hide," and the trainer began to pin it on. Say, I could have killed that trainer. He run that safety pin about an inch into my spine, and I jumped into the air about four feet, and I was going to use a cuss word that I learned in Philadelphia, but I had presence of mind enough to grunt just as Dennis used to, and chatter like a monkey, and the day was saved. The tail was on and I turned my back to show that it was on straight, like a woman's hat, when pa said to hurry the performance to a conclusion, because he could see that there was a spirit of unrest in the audience, and he would not be surprised any moment to see Virginia secede and go out of the union.

There was nothing more for me to do except to drink my cup of after-dinner coffee, and smoke my cigarette, and quit, and I was patting myself on the back at my success and squirming around in the chair, 'cause the pin in my tail hurt my back but I never said a word. The attendant brought in the coffee and I took a couple of swallows, when I realized that somebody had put cayenne pepper into it, and I was hot under the collar, but though I was burning up inside, I never peeped, but just choked and took a swallow of water and vowed to kill the person that made the coffee.

I kept my temper till the trainer handed me the cigarette and a match, and the first puff I realized that they had filled the cigarette with snuff, and after blowing out the smoke I began to sneeze, and the audience fairly went wild. I sneezed about eight times, and at every sneeze the pin in my spine hurt like thunder, but I never lost my temper, till about the seventh sneeze, when my monkey mask flew off, and then a boy about my size, right in front of me, yelled: "It ain't a monkey at all, it is a little nigger," and he threw a ripe persimmon and hit me right in the eye. I said right out in plain English: "You're a liar and I can knock the stuffing out of you."

I pulled off my dress coat and started for him, but pa grabbed me on one side and the monkey trainer on the other, and they tried to get me to return to the monkey character, and chatter, and pa put my monkey mask on me, but I struck right there, and pulled it off, and told him and the managers that I would not play monkey any more with a tail pinned to my spine, my stomach full of cayenne pepper and my nostrils full of Scotch snuff, and my face all puckered up with persimmons.

The crowd yelled: "Fraud! Fraud! Kill the bald-headed old man who is the father of the monkey." and they were making a rush to clean out the show when the dressing-room door opened to let the hippodrome chariot racers out, and the way the chariots scattered the crowd was a caution.

That saved us from serious trouble, for the chariots run over a lot of negroes, which pleased the audience, and they let us off without killing us. They got me back to the dressing-room and had to take a pair of pinchers to get that safety pin out of my spine, and on the way to the dressing-room some one walked on my monkey tail and pulled it off, and that was a dead loss. Pa sat by me and fanned me, 'cause I was faint, and then he said: "My boy, you played your part well, until the persimmon hit you, and then you forgot that you were an actor, and became yourself, and I don't blame you for wanting to punch that boy who called you a little nigger, and said I was your pa. After this chariot race is over we will go around in front of the seats, and find the boy, and you can do him up. Your monkey business was the feature of the show to-day."

We went out and found a boy that looked like the one that sassed me, but he must have been his big brother, 'cause when I went up to him and swatted him on the nose, he gave me a black eye, and I am a sight.

That evening, at the performance, we cut out the educated ourang outang, and the lawyer we met on the cars came to the show, and said we would all be arrested for not performing all we advertised, but he could settle it for a hundred dollars, and pa paid him the money, and he went out and got a jag and came in the show and was going to make trouble, when pa took him to the cage where the 40-foot boa constrictor was uncoiling itself, and the Virginian got one look at the snake and went through the side of the tent yelling: "I've got 'em again. Catch me, somebody."

We got out of town before morning, and nobody was arrested, except the negroes that got run over in the chariot race.

CHAPTER XIX.

The Circus People Visit a Southern Plantation--Pa, the Giant and the
Fat Woman Are Chased by Bloodhounds--The Bad Boy "Runs the
Gauntlet."

Gee, but pa is sore at me. He has been disgusted with me before, but he
never had it in for me so serious as he has now. I guess the whole show
would breathe easier if I should fall off the train some dark night, when
it was stormy, and we were crossing a high bridge over a stream that was
out of its banks on account of a freshet.

It was all on account of our taking an afternoon off on a Sunday at Richmond.
An old planter that used to be in the circus business before the war thought it would
bring back old recollections to him and give us a taste of country life in the south if
he invited all of us, performers, managers, freaks, and everything, to spend the day
on his plantation, and go nutting for chestnuts and hickory nuts, pick apples and
run them through a cider mill and drink self-made cider, and have a good time.

We all appreciated the invitation, and after breakfast we rode out in the country to his plantation in carriages and express wagons and began to do the plantation.
The fat lady and the midgets rode out together in a load of cotton, and when they
got to the house they had to be picked like ducks, and they looked as though they
had been tarred and feathered.

The planter gave us a fine luncheon of fried chicken and corn pone, and cider,
and pa acted as the boss of the circus folks, while the planter and his family, with
about 100 negroes, passed things around. They all seemed to be interested in seeing

how much stuff the giant and the fat lady could hold without putting up sideboards to keep the food from falling off. If pa hadn't told the negroes not to feed the fat lady and the giant any more, there would have been two circus funerals next day.

I got acquainted with a boy that was the planter's son, and while the rest were eating and drinking the boy showed me a pack of hounds that are kept for trailing criminals and negroes who have looked sassy at white women. The trouble with negroes is that they all look alike, and if one commits a crime they can prove an alibi, 'cause every last negro will swear that at the time the crime was committed the suspected man was attending a prayer meeting, so they have to have hounds that can be taken to the place where the crime was committed, and they find the negro's track, and they follow it till they tree him. The hounds do not bite the negro, like we used to hear about, but they just follow him till he is treed, and then they bark, as much as to say: "Ah, there, Mr. Nigger, you just stay where you are till the sheriff comes to fetch you," and Mr. Negro just turns pale and stays on a limb till the sheriff comes with his lynching tools. When the sheriff pulls a gun the negro confesses right there, and the deputy sheriff brings the rope.

I asked the boy if the hounds would trail a white man without hurting him, and he said if you put anise seed on their shoes the hounds will trail 'em all right, so we put up a job to have some fun. The boy gave me some anise seed, and told me to put it on the shoes of anybody I wanted trailed, and after they got out in the woods he would put the hounds on the trail, and the people would have to get up trees, or have their pants chewed, but the dogs would not hurt anybody.

Well, it made me laugh to think about it. I went to pa and told him his shoes were all covered with red Virginia dust, and I took my handkerchief and dusted them off, and made him hold up his foot like a horse that is being shod. Then I put a handful of anise seed around the sole, and in his shoes. He said it was mighty kind in me to do it. Then I went to the giant, and brushed the dust off his shoes, and put two handfuls of anise seed in them, and he said I was a nice boy. I told the fat woman about the dust on her telescope valises, and I rubbed it off, and gave her feet a dose of anise seed that ought to have paralyzed a pack of hounds. She wanted to hug me and let me kiss her, but I said I passed, and she said she would do as much for me some time.

About this time the planter took the lead, and they all went across a pasture into the woods, and began knocking nuts off the trees. All through the woods there were signs: "No Tresspassing," and "Beware of the Dogs," but the planter said to never mind the signs. I told the boy to let the dogs loose on the trail in about half an hour, and I went along with the folks, and I told pa I had seen a pack of blood-hounds that would eat people alive, and if he heard hounds barking to run like a whitehead and climb a tree. I got with the giant, who is a coward in his own right, and told him the only trouble about these great plantations in the south was the wild dogs that inhabited the mountains, that would not hesitate to attack a man if they got good and hungry, but there was no danger to him, because he was a good sprinter, and could outrun a jack rabbit. The giant wanted to go back to the house, 'cause he said he didn't want to run no foot race with hounds, and he had seen the sign to beware of the dogs. I never ought to have done it, 'cause the fat woman looks as though she was built a purpose for apoplexy, but I told her as a friend, not to load herself down with nuts, but to travel light, so if the wild dogs came down to raid the plantation she could crawl in a hole out of sight till the dogs had eaten some of the men. She came near fainting right there, before the dogs got busy.

There were about 20 negroes throwing clubs at the nuts, and everybody was having a big time. The trapeze performers were squirreling up among the limbs, when suddenly, in the distance came the bay of the pack of bloodhounds, and every negro turned pale, and got ready to climb a tree. The planter stopped to listen, and when one of the managers of the show asked him what was the matter, he said: "You can search me, sah. If that is my pack of hounds a crime has been committed, and the sheriff has started the pack on the trail of the criminal, sah, because the dogs are never turned loose, except for business."

Then the planter yelled to the niggers, and said: "If any of youall are guilty of crime, you best get scarce, or pick out your tree, and get up it mighty sudden, 'cause the hounds haven't been fed lately." Every colored man picked a tree, and the hounds kept coming, finally showing up jumping the fence, and entering the woods, and the planter cut a club to beat off the dogs. Pa looked as innocent as John Wanamaker's picture addressing a Sunday school, the giant saw the dogs and started for a tall tree, and the fat lady said she couldn't find any hole big enough to hide in, and "the idea," if there were not men enough to protect a lady.

Well, I never expected to see anything so fine as the way those hounds run with their noses to the ground, scattered in three packs one pack on the trail of each of the three whose shoes I had doctored. When they got near us they broke up and went around everywhere that pa and the giant and the fat lady had walked, and fell over each other, but finally one pack went to the tall tree where the giant had climbed to the first limb, and stood on their hind legs and barked a salute to him. He trembled so I was afraid he would fall off, but he wound his arms and legs around the tree, and began to cry. The planter told him whatever crime he had committed it was all up with him.

The part of the pack that was on pa's trail began to close in on pa, and I said: "Pa, if you don't want to be dog meat, it is up to you to climb, and you better get a move on, or I shall be an orphan mighty quick, 'cause the dogs are starving." Pa made a couple of quick jumps, and grabbed a limb of a hickory tree, and was pulling himself up and repeating prayers, when the leading dog reached up his nose and smelled pa's shoes, when the intelligent animal gave a bark and a yell to the other dogs, as much as to say: "That's the identical cuss. Eat him alive."

He grabbed about a double handful of the cloth of pa's clothes right below where his suspenders button on and held on, and shook pa real hard, but the cloth was tough and didn't tear. Pa suddenly seemed to be endowed with superhuman strength, for he drew himself up on the limb and raised the dog from the ground, and all the pack came around the tree and set up a howl that scared pa so the perspiration rolled off him, and he had a chill so he shook like the ague.

Pa yelled to the planter, who was holding up the fat lady and said: "Here, Mr. Confederate, I am not a union prisoner, and I want you to unlock your dog's jaws, and free me, 'cause I can't hold up a 90-pound dog by my suspenders much longer. If this is southern hospitality, I don't want to be entertained no more." The planter leaned the fat lady against a tree, and took the dog by the hind legs and pulled him off.

The planter yelled to the negroes to come down and help handle the dogs, but just then the boy who started the dogs on the trail, at my request, came up whistling, with a dog whip in his hand, and all the dogs surrounded him, and he made them lay down and roll over. All of the scared people came down from their perches in the trees, and surrounded the boy and the dogs, and the dogs panted and lolled, as though they had been having a nice run for their money. The old planter asked his boy how the dogs had happened to get loose, and that fool boy told the whole thing, how I had asked him to let the pack run, and how I had put anise seed in the shoes of pa, the giant and the fat lady. Then you ought to have seen what they did to me. The planter said they usually had a lynching when the dogs made a run, but that was impossible in this case, so he suggested that they make me run the gauntlet. I didn't know what running the gauntlet was, but after pa had told me he should disown me from that moment, I said I was willing to run any gauntlet, so they all cut switches and formed in two lines, and let me run down between them. I thought it would be fun, but when I started and every last man gave me a cut across the end of my back with a hickory switch, I yelled murder, and run between the giant's legs and tackled him like football I toppled him over against the next man, and that man hit the giant in the stomach, and everybody began to fight, and the festivities broke up.

I went to the house with the boy and the dogs, and we set the dogs on a mess of cats, and treed everything alive on the plantation. Finally the whole crowd came back to the house and had another lunch, with mint julep and champagne, and then everybody was hugging some one, and crying on each other's neck, and swearing that the war was over, and that the north and the south were one and inseparable, and the two together could whip the whole world.

Pa somehow saw double. I was standing alone, smarting from the switching I got, when pa came up to me and said: "I want you two boys to understand that I don't want any more experiments played on me. I can take a joke us well as anybody, but when you set a hundred dogs on my trail, I am no gentlemen, see? Now we will go back to the show."

CHAPTER XX.

The Bad Boy Goes After a Mess of White Turnips for the Menagerie--He Feeds the Animals Horseradish, but Gets the Worst of the Deal.

You can learn something new and interesting every day in a circus, and a boy, particularly, can store his mind with useful knowledge, that will be valuable to him in after years.

Gee, but I have learned some things that I could never have learned in college, 'cause at college you only learn things that have to be verified by actual experience in business. Pa says one year in the circus will be better for me than ten years in a reform school. But I learned something yesterday that made such an impression on me that I will not be able to sit down comfortably before the season is over.

You see, it was this way. Once a week it is the custom to feed all the animals that are vegetarians a mess of ground white turnips, 'cause it opens up the pores, and makes the animals feel good, like a politician who goes to French Lick springs, and has the whisky boiled out of him. After the animals have eaten the turnip mush, they become agreeable, and will rub against the keepers, and eat out of your hand.

I had been with pa a dozen times to find a place where we could get a few barrels of turnips ground up fine, and so yesterday, when the boss animal keeper was sick, and turned his job over to pa, pa told me to go out in town, at Lynchburg, Va., and get a couple of washtubs full of ground turnips, and have the stuff sent in to the menagerie tent in time for the afternoon performance. I got a boy to go with me. We hunted all the groceries and couldn't find turnips enough to make a first payment, but we found a place where they grate horseradish and bottle it for the market, and I ordered two washtubs full of horseradish grated nicely, and sent to the tent, but I made the man bill it as ground turnips.

The boy and I played all the forenoon, and when the man started with the ground horseradish for the tent, we went along, and I introduced the man to pa, and pa O. K.'d the bill, and sent him to the treasurer after the money. I was going to get on a back seat and watch the animals eat, but pa said: "Here, you boys, get out those pans and portion out the turnips and pass 'em around just as the crowd comes in, 'cause after the animals have had a mess of cut feed they are better natured, and show off better."

I was pretty leery about feeding the animals horseradish, and would have preferred to have some one else do it, who did not care to live any longer, but I said: "Yes, sir," just like that, and touched my hat to pa, and he said to the boss canvasman: "There's a boy you can swear by."

The boss canvasman said: "You are right, old man, but if he was mine, I would kill him so quick it would make your head swim," and he and pa went off laughing, but I think they laughed too soon.

Well, we took a spud and put about a quart of horseradish in each pan, and put the pans in front of each animal, and you ought to have seen them rush for the supposed turnips, like a drove of cattle after salt.

The boy and I got up on the platform with the freaks, to be in a safe place, and watch the animals, and see how they digested their food. The first animal to open up the chorus was the hippopotamus, 'cause we gave him about four quarts of horseradish on account of his mouth, and he swallowed it at one mouthful. First he looked as though he felt hurt, and stopped chewing, and seemed to be thinking, like a horse that wakes up in the night with colic, and raises the whole family to sit up with him all night and pour things down his neck out of a long-neck bottle. The hippo held his breath for about a minute, and then he opened his mouth so you could drive a wagon in, and gave the grand hailing sign of distress, and said: "Wow, wow, wow," as plain as a man could. Then he rolled over into his tank and yelled "murder," and wallowed around, and stood on his head, till one of the keepers went in the cage to try to soothe him. He chased the keeper out, and the crowd that had just begun to come in fell back in terror.

There was quite a crowd around the camels watching them peacefully chew their cuds, as they do at evening on the dessert, and the Arabs who had charge of the camels were standing around, posing as though they were the whole thing, when the old black, double-hump camel got his quart of horseradish down into one of his stomachs, as he was kneeling down on all fours. He yelled: "O, mamma," and got up on all his feet, and kicked an Arab off a prayer rug, and bellowed and groaned. Then the rest of the herd of camels seemed to have swallowed their dose, and they made Rome howl. This scared the people over to where the sacred cattle were trying to set a pious example to the rest of the animals by their meek and lowly conduct.

The sacred cow got her horseradish first, and I could see she was trying to hold it without giving the snap away, till her husband, the bull, got his. Well, it was pitiful, and I made up my mind I would never play a joke on the sacred cattle again, 'cause it seems like sacrilege. The bull finally got his horseradish down, and he was the most astonished animal I ever saw. He swelled up, and then bellowed until the cow looked as though she would sink through the ground, saying; "Excuse me, dear, but I am not to blame, because I, too, have a hot box." The bull acted just as human as could be, 'cause he looked mad at her, and was going to gore her to death, when pa and some of the hands came up and hit him with a tent stake, and swore at him, and he quit fighting his wife, just like a man. Pa wanted to know what in thunder was the matter with the animals, and wanted to know if I had fed them the turnips, and I told him they had all been fed, and just then the giraffe, whose neck was so long the horseradish did not reach a vital spot as quick as it did with the hippo, began to yell for the police and dance around. Finally he stood on his head and neck, with his heels against a cage, and coughed like he had caught pneumonia. Pa said to the boss canvasman: "Well, what do you think of that?"

The zebras had their inning next, and after they had swallowed their rations of horseradish, they never said a word, but began to run around like dancing the lancers, and when they got to going it looked like a kaleidoscope, and the six zebras looked like a million. Pa said: "I never saw such a sight since I used to drink, but I have either got the jim-jams, or something awful has happened to this menagerie."

The educated hog got a double dose, and he squealed and couldn't pick out the right card, and then the llamas got busy on their portion of horseradish, and they cried in Spanish, and stood on their hind legs and shed tears. Pa got so rattled he looked ten years older than he did when the afternoon performance opened. The manager of the big show came in to know why the elephants had not been sent into the dressing-room, to be got ready for the grand entree. Just then the elephants began to eat their horseradish, and when they were driven into the big tent they were complaining about something being wrong inside of them, and as they came by the lemonade stand they seemed to be yelling "Fire!" Then they all stopped at the stand and began to drink the lemonade out of the barrels, which seemed to put out the fire.

The animals quieted down a little, and pa went into the big tent to consult the manager, and I thought it was a shame that the lions and hyenas and tigers couldn't have any fun, so I went to the table where the meat was laid out ready to feed them, and cut a hole in each piece of meat and put in a double handful of horseradish, and just then the feeder came along and began to throw the meat in the cages. Gee, but those carnivorous animals are bad enough even if you give them nice boiled sirloin steak, and they fight enough over it, at any time, but when they began to chew and tear the meat, and get horseradish hot from the griddle, they didn't do a thing. The audience thought the animals would kill everybody. The big lion got his meat down, but it didn't set well, and he turned a somersault, and snarled, and pulled the bars of the cage, while the grizzly bear rolled up in a ball and rolled over in his cage till the men had to hold on to the wheels to keep the shebang from going over. The hyenas, who are always mad, went on a tear that could be heard in all the tents.

Pa and the managers came back into the menagerie tent with the animal keeper, who had been sent for, and they began to try to find out what ailed the animals, and the animal keeper asked what pa had been feeding them, and pa said he had given them their ground turnips.

"Turnips, indeed," said the keeper, as he took up some of the turnip and tasted of it, and he handed a handful to pa. Pa tasted it, and pa had a hot box, and the managers tasted of it, and they said: "No wonder." Then they asked pa where he got it, and pa said he sent me to order it, and then they all said: "That settles it."

I thought I would go 'way and jump in the river, but pa said: "Hennery, come here, my angel," and he spit on his hands and picked up a barrel stave. I went right up to pa, as innocent as could be, just as any dutiful son should, and right there before the animals and freaks pa--well, that's the reason I am not sitting down very much these days. So long.

CHAPTER XXI.

The Bad Boy and His Pa Inject a Little Politics Into the Show--Rival Bands of Atlanta Citizens Meet in the Circus Tent--A Bunch of Angry Hornets Causes Much Bitter Feeling.

I expect that next year I shall be one of the managers of this show, 'cause they tell me I have got the greatest head of any boy that has ever traveled with the show.

We haven't been having a very big business in the south, because the negroes haven't money enough to patronize shows, and a lot of the white people are either too high-toned or else they are politicians and want a pass. The managers and heads of departments held a meeting to devise some way to get both classes interested, and everybody was asked to state their views. After they all got through talking pa asked me what I thought would be the best way to get the people excited about the show, and I told him there was no way except to inject a little politics into it. I said if they would give me $50 or so, to buy Chinese lanterns, and about a hundred complimentary tickets to give away, pa and I could go to Atlanta a couple of days ahead of the show and we could organize a Roosevelt club among the negroes, and a Bryan club among the white fellows, and at the evening performance we could have the two clubs march into the main tent, one from the main entrance, and one from the dressing room, with Chinese lanterns, and one could yell for Roosevelt and the other for Bryan, and advertise that a great sensation would be sprung at the evening performance. I said the tent wouldn't begin to hold the people.

Every one of the managers and heads of departments said it would be great stuff. Pa was the only one that kicked. He said the two processions might get into a fight, but I said what if they did, we wouldn't be to blame. Let 'em fight if they want to, and we can see fair play.

So they all agreed that pa and I should go to Atlanta ahead, and organize the political processions, and, say, we had such a time that the circus came near never getting out of the town alive. We overdid the thing, so they wanted to lynch me, and pa wanted to help.

The way it was was this way: Pa was to organize the white men for Bryan, and I was to organize the negroes for Roosevelt, and we went to work and bought 600 Chinese lanterns, and pa stored his half of the lanterns in a barn on the circus lot and I stored mine in another barn owned by a negro that I gave five dollars to be my assistant, with a promise that he should have a job traveling with the show, to milk the sacred cow. I told this negro what the program was, and that I wanted 200 negroes who had an ambition to be politicians, and hold office, and I would not only pass them into the show free, but see that they got a permanent office. What we had got to do, I said, was to stampede the white procession, that would be led by pa, and the way to do it was for every negro in my party to skirmish around in the woods and find a hornet's nest, and bring it to our barn, and fit it into one of the Chinese lanterns, and fix a candle on top of the nest, while the hornets were asleep. Then when we met the Bryan procession we were to shout and wave our lanterns, and if necessary to whack the white men over the head with the lantern with the hornets' nest, and the hornets would wake up and do the rest.

The negro wanted to know how I could prevent the hornets from stinging our own men, and I told him that we had been in the hornet business all the season and never had one of our own men stung. I said we took some assafoetida and rubbed it on our clothes and faces, and the hornets wouldn't touch us, but just went for the other fellows to beat the band. Say, negroes are easy marks. You can make them believe anything. But if I ever get to be president I am going to appoint my negro assistant to a position in my cabinet, 'cause he is the greatest political organizer I ever saw. He rounded up over 200 cotton pickers and negro men who work in the freight depots once in a while and started them out after hornets' nests. He gave them some change to get a drink, and promised them free passes into the show next night, and the next morning they showed up with hornets' nests enough to scare you. They put them in a dark place in the barn, so the hornets wouldn't get curious and want to come out of the nests before they got their cue.

That afternoon we fitted them into the Chinese lanterns, and tied sticks on the lanterns and fixed the candles, and when night came there were more negroes than I could use, But I told them to follow along, and the door tender would let them in, and all they need to do was to yell for Teddy when I did, and so we marched to the main tent about the time the performance got to going. I saw pa with his gang of white men go into the dressing room at about the same time. The manager had timed it for us to come in about 8:30, into the main tent, when the elephants were in their pyramid act, so my crowd of negroes stopped in the menagerie tent half an hour waiting to be called.

I wish I wasn't so confounded curious, but I suppose I was born that way. I took one of the Chinese lanterns that was not lighted and just thought I would like to see what the hyenas and the big lion, who were in the same cage, with an iron partition between them, would do if a Chinese lantern was put in the cage, so I got the fellow that watches the cage to open up the top trap door, and I dropped a Chinese lantern with a hornets' nest in it right between the two hyenas. Gee, but you ought to have seen them pounce on it, and bite it and tear it up, and then the hornets woke up, and they didn't do a thing to that mess of hyenas. The hyenas set up a grand hailing sign of distress, and howled pitiful, and the lion raised up his head and looked at them through the bars as though he was saying, in a snarling way, "What you grave robbers howling about? Can't you keep still and let the czar of all the animals enjoy his after dinner nap?"

Just then the hyenas kicked what was left of the hornets' nest under the bars into his side of the cage, and he put his foot on it and growled, and about a hundred hornets gave him his. He gave an Abyssinian cough that woke all the animals, and then the hornets scattered and before I knew it the zebras were dancing a snake dance and all of them were howling as though they were in the ark, hungry, and the ark had landed on Mount Ararat.

Just then one of the assistant managers beckoned to me to lead in my procession and we lighted the candles in our Chinese lanterns. I didn't stop to see how the animals got along with the hornets, but I couldn't help thinking that if one hornets' nest could raise such a row, what would a hundred or so do when we got to going in the other tent?

Oh, if I had only died when I was young, I never would have witnessed that sight. The band played, "There'll be a Hot Time in the Old Town To-night," and pa's crowd of white trash marched around the big outside ring shouting, "Bryan! Bryan! What's the matter with Bryan!" and the audience got up on its hind legs and yelled--that is the white folks did--and then we marched around the other way, and yelled, "Teddy is the stuff! Teddy is the stuff!" and the negroes in the audience yelled. Then my crowd met pa's crowd right by the middle ring, where the elephants had formed the pyramid that closes their act, and the Japanese jugglers were in the right-hand ring, and a party of female tumblers, with low-necked stockings, were standing at attention in the left-hand ring.

There was no intention of having a riot, but when pa yelled, "What's the matter with Bryan?" a negro in my crowd yelled, "That's what's the matter with Bryan," and he hit pa over the head with his Chinese lantern, loaded with a warm hornets' nest as big as a football, which had taken fire from the candle. Pa dropped his lantern and began to fight hornets, and then all the white trash in pa's bunch rushed up and began to whack my poor downtrodden negroes with their Chinese lanterns. Of course, my fellows couldn't stand still and be mauled, and the candles had warmed our hornets' nests so the hornets were crawling out to see what was the trouble. Then every negro whacked a white man with a hornets' nest and the audience fairly went wild with excitement.

The hornets got busy and went for the elephants and the Japanese jugglers, and they stampeded like they never met a hornet before.

The female tumblers found hornets on their stockings, and everywhere, and they gave a female war whoop and rushed for the dressing room. The elephants got stung and they came down off their pyramid and went out to the menagerie tent trumpeting, and switching their trunks. The negroes and the white politicians were getting into a race war, so the circus hands rushed in and separated them, and my negroes found that the fetty I had them rub on themselves did not keep the hornets from stinging them, so they stampeded.

Then the hornets began to go for the audience, and the women yelled murder and pulled down their dresses to cover their shoes, and the men got stung and the whole audience stampeded into the open air.

Then I met pa, and he was a sight, and I never got stung once. The managers tried to get the band to play some tune that would soothe and hold the audience till an explanation could be made, but somebody had thrown a hornets' nest under the band seats and the horn players got stung on the lips so they couldn't play, and the band all lit out for a beer garden. Before I realized it the show was over, and a detective that detects for the show had me collared and brought me up before a meeting of the managers. Pa was the prosecuting attorney, and told them that I didn't run my politics fair, 'cause I had brought in a lot of ringers. The managers asked me how the hornets' nests came to be in the Chinese lanterns. I told them they would have to ask the negroes for how was I to know what weapons they had concealed about their persons, any more than pa was responsible if his politicians carried revolvers.

They said that looked reasonable, but they believed I knew more about it than anybody, but as we had to pack up the show and make the next town they wouldn't lynch me till the next day. Pa got me to put cold cream on his stings, and then he said, "Hennery, you are the limit."

CHAPTER XXII.

The Show Does Poor Business in the South--Pa Side Tracks a Circus
Car Filled with Creditors--A Performance Given "For the Poor," Fills
the Treasury--A Wild West Man Buncoes the Show.

Gee, but this show has been up against it the last week. We haven't made
a paying stand anywhere. The show business is all right when you have
to turn people away, or let them in on standing room. Then you can snap
your fingers at fate, and drink foolish water out of four-dollar bottles of
fizz that has the cork trained so it will pop out clear to the top of the tent, and make
a noise that makes you think you own the earth, but when you strike the southern
country where the white men have not sold their cotton and the negroes have not
been paid for picking it, the audience looks like a political caucus in an off year,
when there is nobody with money enough to stimulate the voters. When the audiences are small, and half the people in attendance get in on bill-sticker's passes, and
you can't pay the help regularly, but have to stand them off with promises, you are
liable to have a strike any minute. The people you owe for hotel bills, and horse
feed, and supplies, follow you from one town to another, threatening to attach the
ticket wagon and levy on the animals. It takes diplomacy and unadulterated gall to
run a show.

We are playing now to get back into the northern states, but we have to leave
an animal of some kind in the hands of a sheriff every day, which has been all right
so far, 'cause we have steered the sheriffs on to elephants that have corns so they are
no good except to eat, one zebra that was made up by a painter, who painted stripes
on a white mule, and one lion that was so old he will never sell at forced sale for
enough to pay for the beef tea the sheriff will have to feed him.

When creditors in a town get too mad and threaten to attach things, we invite them to go along with us for a few days, and get their money when we strike a paying stand, and we agree to furnish them a Pullman car and all they can eat. That is rather tempting to country people, so we had a full car load of creditors with us for a week, and we gave them plenty to drink, so they had the time of their lives, but they didn't get their money. After going with us all through Georgia, they held an indignation meeting in the car, and between high balls and cheese sandwiches they got sleepy, and we side tracked their car in the woods at a station in Mississippi, where there was a post office, saw mill and a cotton gin. I guess they are there yet unless Mr. Pullman's lost car experts have found the car and driven them out with fire extinguishers.

Pa came pretty near being left in that car with the creditors in Mississippi. He was helping to entertain the guests, and jollying them up to believe they would get their money when we got to Memphis the next day, when he noticed the car had been sidetracked, and he knew that was the way we were going to dispose of the creditors. He thought some one would tell him when to get off, but he was sitting up with a landlady from some place in Georgia that we owed a lot of money for feeding the freaks, and she was threatening that if she didn't get her money she would have the heart's blood of some one. So pa was afraid to leave for fear she would stab him.

But when the car stopped on the siding, pa took off his coat and hat and yawned, and said he guessed he would turn in, and she let him go to his berth, and he got out on the platform, and just then the second section of our train came along, and stopped for water, and pa crawled into an animal car and laid down in the straw with the sacred cow. She bellowed all night 'cause the sacred bull, her husband, had been attached for debt at Vicksburg, but when pa got in the car in his shirt sleeves and humped his shoulders up on account of the cold, the cow thought maybe she had been unnecessarily alarmed, and maybe pa was her husband.

So she quit bellowing, and laid down and chewed her cud till daylight. Then when she saw that pa was another person she got mad and chased him up into the rafters of the car, and he had to ride there until the train got to Memphis. The hands rescued pa, but he got away from the creditors all right.

We made a new lot of creditors at Memphis, and they proposed to go along with us, but we shook them off.

Gee, but we made a killing in Memphis, and don't you forget it. We had hand-bills on all the wagons in the parade, telling the people that the proceeds of the afternoon and evening performance would be given to deserving persons, in char-ity, and the intention was to use the money to pay off the hands. My, but how the people turned out. The tents were all full, and we had more money than we have had in a month before, and after the performance at night the mayor and some prominent citizens waited on the management and asked when and where we were going to distribute the money to the deserving persons.

The managers appointed pa to stand off the committee. Pa said he had noticed, in walking about the city, a beautiful park in the center of the town, and he told the committee that his idea was to have the deserving people gather at the park the next morning, which was Sunday, and wait there until the managers of the show could count the money, and prepare to distribute it, honestly and impartially, with the advice of the local committee. That seemed all right, and the committee noti-fied the citizens to meet in the park at nine o'clock the next morning, and receive the money the citizens had so kindly contributed to such a noble cause, and they went away.

Our show has got out of a good many tight places, but we never got out of a town so quietly and unostentatiously as we got out of Memphis during that early Sunday morning. There was not noise enough made getting our stuff to the train to wake up a policeman, and before daylight the different sections of the train had crossed the big bridge into Arkansas, and were on the way to the Indian Territory. Pa and the other managers were on the platform of the last car of the last section, as it pulled out across the river, at daylight, and even that early it seemed as though the whole colored population of Memphis was on the way to the park, to secure good positions, so they could receive their share of the money. As the train got to the middle of the river, and safe into Arkansas, the whole management breathed a sigh of relief. The boss canvasman said: "It is like getting money from home," and pa said: "It is like taking money from the tin cup of a blind organ grinder," and the treasurer of the show said, as he put the day's receipts in the safe in the business car: "It looks good to me." Then they all turned in to sleep the happy hours away, that beautiful Sunday on the way to Indian Territory and Oklahoma.

Well, sir, you can never make me believe that money obtained dishonestly will stay by a person, or do him any good, and that was demonstrated in the case of our show the next day. We got acquainted with an old showman who was out of luck, who used to run a wild west show, but got busted up, and as he didn't care where he went, we took him with us on the train, and all day Sunday he talked about his show experiences, and finally he said if we had any horses with our show that could run races, we could make a barrel of money at Guthrie, where we were to make our next stand. He said the Indians and half breeds all had Indian ponies that they thought could beat any horses that ever wore shoes, and that they would bet every cent they had on their ponies, and as they had just been paid their annuities by the government, they had money in bales, and we could get it all, if we had horses that were any good, and money to back them. His idea was to give out that owing to some accident we could not give an afternoon performance, and just get out the horses and bet the Indians to a standstill, and win all their money, and give a free evening show as a sort of consolation to the Indians.

Well, it looked good to pa, and he talked to the other managers, and the result was when we got to Guthrie we had made up our minds that as money was what we were after, the easiest way was to get it by racing our horses.

So when we got settled in Guthrie, and got the tent up, we announced that part of the show was in a wreck down the road in Arkansas, and we should have to abandon the afternoon performance, but in the meantime there would be a little horse racing on the side, if anybody in Oklahoma had any horses they thought could run some.

Well, I thought there were Indians and ponies and squaws enough before the announcement was made, but in less than two hours more than a thousand ponies were being brought in, and we got our chariot racers, and our bareback hippodrome horses, and they were being led around and admired, and we all laughed at the little runts of Indian ponies, and the Indians got mad and backed their ponies.

Pretty soon the races began in the vacant lot just outside the town. The old showman we had brought up from Memphis was made master of ceremonies, 'cause he could talk Choctaw, and Comanche, and other Indian jargon, and things got busy. The Indians wouldn't run their ponies more than an eighth of a mile, or a quarter, and we consented, because the poor little things didn't look as though they could run a block, they were so thin, and sleepy. Pa was afraid the humane society would have us arrested for cruelty to animals. All our fellows were provided with money, and they flashed rolls of bills in the faces of the Indians, and finally Mr. Indian would reach down under his clothes and pull out a roll, and wet his thumb and peel off big bills, and before we knew it we were investing a fortune in the racing game. Then the racing began, and the horses were sent off at the drop of a hat, or the firing of a pistol.

I was given some money to bet with the little Indians, 'cause pa said we wanted to get every dollar in the tribe, for if we didn't get it the Indians would spend it for fire water. The first race was between one of our best runners and a sleepy little spotted pony, and when the hat was dropped the pony made a few jumps and was off like a rabbit, and our horse couldn't see him for the dust, and our horse was distanced. The next race resulted the same, and all day long we never won a race, and the Indians took our money and put it in their pants and never smiled. The old showman we had befriended seemed crushed.

When our money was nearly all gone to the confounded Indians, and the sun was going down, he went up to pa and said: "Uncle, what does this all mean? I thought your horses could run."

Pa said: "Damfino, I never was no horse racer, nohow."

When our money was all gone, and our horses were nearly dead from fatigue, the managers all got together in the big tent for a consultation on finances, and it was the saddest sight I ever saw. Pa tried to be cheerful, and he said: "Well, we will give the evening performance, and when the Indians are all in the tent we can turn out the lights and turn the boys loose on them, and maybe they will find some of the money in their breech clouts."

"You don't mean to rob them, do you?" said the boss canvasman, and pa said: "No, no; far from it. We will borrow it of them. It is no harm to borrow from an Indian."

Just then the treasurer came in with an empty tin box he had carried the money out in, and he said there would be no use of having an evening performance, 'cause the Indians had taken their ponies and squaws and money and gone towards the setting sun, and pa said: "Where is that old showman?" and the treasurer said: "He has gone with them. He is their legal adviser, and went down to Memphis to rope us into the game."

CHAPTER XXIII.

The Circus Has Bad Luck in Indian Territory--A Herd of Animals Turned Out to Graze Is Stampeded by Indians--They Go Dashing Over the Plains, and the Circus Tent Follows, Picked Up by a Cyclone. No more horse racing for this circus.

The managers held a meeting at Guthrie, Okla., after we had lost our money horse racing with the Indians, and pa said the consensus of opinion was that we better stick to the legitimate show business, and not try to work in any side lines. Pa says he made a speech at the managers' meeting, in which he showed that the business man who attended strictly to the business which he knew all about, would make money, while the man who knew about dry goods, but worked in a millinery store or a stock of tinware, got it in the neck. He would either get stuck on the head milliner, or buy a stock of tinware that would not hold water.

So a resolution was passed to the effect that hereafter no temptation could be great enough to get our show to go into anything outside of the business, no matter how good it looked as a get-rich-quick affair. So we gathered up our show and played a whole week in Oklahoma, and had full houses all the time, and made money enough to redeem our animals that had been attached by creditors. We have paid up our debts, and we got out of Oklahoma with flying colors.

If we had gone right on to Kansas we would have shown sense, but some cowboys from the Indian Territory told pa and the other managers that if we would take the show to the Indian Territory we couldn't get cars enough to haul the money away, as the Indians had got round-shouldered and bow-legged carrying the money they had made grazing cattle, and the territory was full of cowboys that had money to burn, and they hadn't seen a circus since the war.

Well, it seemed a shame to go by the Indian Territory, and allow those poor Indians to break their backs carrying money around, and so we sent a carload of bill pasters into the territory and billed towns that would hold us about a week, and we figured that we would clean up enough money to last us all a life-time. I wish I didn't have to write about the result, 'cause we are broke up so we can't look pleasant to have our pictures taken.

It was a bright, beautiful Sunday morning that we arrived at Muskoka, and soon after daylight we had our tents pitched. As we had all day Sunday to rest, pa suggested that it would be a good idea to take all our animals that eat grass out on the grazing ground on the edge of the town and let them fill up on the nice blue grass that was knee-high all over the country. So after breakfast we detailed men to take charge of the different animals, and herd them out in the tall grass. It was a beautiful sight to see those rare animals, gathered from all over the world, eating grass together, in perfect peace, in this new country. The animals that we thought would stand without hitching, like the elephants, were cared for by their attendants, but the animals that might wander from their own fireside, were picketed out, or held by long ropes, the deer, the buffalo, the zebras, the sacred cattle, the elk, the yaks, the camels and that kind, were tied with long lariats, and held by the men detailed by the managers. For a couple of hours the animals just gorged themselves, after they had kicked up their heels a spell and rolled in the grass. Then one of the elephants got up on his hind feet and held up two toes, like boys in school hold up two fingers when they want to go in swimming, and the elephant started for a creek and went in the water, and the whole herd followed, and they spattered each other, and ducked and rolled around just like school boys. The whole population of the town, whites and Indians, came to the bank of the river to watch the fun.

Pa was holding his elk by a rope and one of the managers had a rope around the neck of a giraffe: the treasurer and the ticket taker was leading the zebras, and everybody was busy with some kind of animal, and I had a rope around an antelope, and some of our men on horseback were herding the buffaloes. It didn't seem as though anything wrong could happen. The elephants wouldn't come out of the creek, so the boss canvasman went over to where there were about 500 cowboys and Indians on horseback, and asked them to ride into the creek and drive the elephants out where the rest of the animals were, on the prairie.

Gee, but that was the greatest mistake he could have made. The men on horseback didn't want any better fun, so they made a charge, in line of battle, just like Sheridan's cavalry, down the bank, into the creek, yelling and waving lariat ropes, and snapping whips and the elephants got out of that creek in a hurry. The cowboys threw lassoes over the hind feet of the elephants, and tried to hold them, and the elephants bellowed, and dragged the cowboys and their ponies right amongst the other animals, and in about a minute, as the boss canvasman said when he came to, and they were picking the cactus thorns out of him: "Hell was just plumb out for noon."

The buffaloes smelled the Indians, and they started to stampede, like they used to do when they lived on the plains, and all the animals followed, dragging the men who had hold of their ropes, and away we all went over a rise of ground, the zebras in the lead and the elephants fetching up the rear, the cowboys and Indians behind, yelling and ki-i-ing, and more than 500 Indian dogs barking.

Well, pa was the foolishest man in the lot, 'cause he had tied the lariat rope that he held his elk by, around his belt, and when the elk went over the hill pa was only hitting the high places, and he was yelling for me to head off his elk. But I was busy trying to keep up with my antelope, which was scared worse than any animal in the race. When the antelope and I overtook the boss canvasman, who was digging his heels into the ground trying to hold his zebra, I thought it was a good time to say something pleasant, so I said: "This is a lovely country we are passing through," but I never heard his reply, 'cause just then the zebra jumped over a big cactus and the boss canvasman went into it, and stayed there, yelling for a piece of ice, while the zebras that were dragging the treasurer and the ticket taker passed us. I yelled to the treasurer and told him I should have to have my salary raised if I was expected to keep up with my antelope, but he told me where to go to get an increase of salary, some place in Arkansas--maybe Hot Springs.

Then my antelope heard the Indians and cowboys coming behind, and he got his second wind, and I never did touch the ground no more, and I must have looked like a buzzard sailing through the air. When my antelope got up to where pa was trying to keep up with his elk. I told pa he better let go his elk and get the cowboys and Indians to ride around ahead of the stampede and head them off.

Pa said he couldn't let go of his elk 'cause the rope was tied to his belt, but for me to hit the ground somewhere ahead and let go of that jack rabbit I was chasing, and tell the cowboys to head off the stampede. So when I lit again I let go the rope, and the antelope got ahead of everything, and I wished I had bet on him.

When the cowboys and Indians got up to me I delivered the message from pa, and they divided and went around the flanks of the stampeders, and in another mile they headed them off in a nice pasture, and kept riding around the animals so they couldn't get away. They soon had the whole bunch under control, and we all got together to see if anybody was hurt.

Well, pa was the worst sight of all If his belt had broke he never would have lost his pants, 'cause more than a million cactus thorns had gone through and pinned them on. We had to cut them off, and pull out the thorns with pincers, one at a time, and pa yelling murder for every thorn. The boss canvasman was in the same fix, and everybody that tried to hold an animal was pinned together with thorns, and they had gravel up their trousers from sticking their heels into the soil.

Everybody was mad and they threatened to lynch pa when they got back to the tent for suggesting letting the animals out to graze. We started back to town, the cowboys and Indians driving the animals, and the zebras and giraffes kicking up and acting as though they had got out of school on account of the death of a dear teacher, like schoolboys. Before we got to town a wind came up so strong that we had to walk edgewise to go against it, and finally we met the tent coming out to meet us, 'cause a cyclone had taken it bodily and was blowing it all over the prairie. And when we got to town the animals in the cages, that can't eat grass, were having an indignation meeting, and howling awful.

Pa was the first man to get back to the lot, and he asked me what I thought he better do, and I told him he better get in the porcupine cage, 'cause he looked, with the cactus thorns sticking out of him, like the father of all porcupines. He said I thought I was smart, and he asked me if I was hurt any, and I told him all I could find was a stone bruise on my spine where I struck a prairie dog house.

Well, we got the animals into a livery barn, and it took us almost the whole week to have the tent hauled back and sewed together, and we had to pay the cowboys and Indians more than the animals were worth to bring them back, and let them into the show free. The managers had a meeting and resolved to get out of the Indian Territory and into Kansas just as quick as possible.

CHAPTER XXIV.

Pa Is Sent to a Hospital to Recuperate--The Bad Boy Discourages
Other Boys from Running Away with the Circus--He Makes Them Water
the Camels, Curry the Hyenas and Put Insect Powder on the Buffaloes.

This is the first time since we started out with the circus in the spring that pa and I have not been two "Johnnies on the spot," ready for anything that the managers told us to do. Oklahoma, though, and the Indian Territory, have been too much for pa, and they sent him on to Kansas City to recuperate in a hospital for a week, while the show does Kansas to a finish, and makes a triumphal entry into Missouri.

I wonder how the show will get along without us for a week, 'cause they sentenced me to go along with pa, so I could be handy to hold his hands when the doctors are pulling cactus needles out of his hide. I guess pa was willing enough to jump Kansas in the night from what he told us once.

He said when he was a young man he and a railroad brakeman got busted at Topeka, and they had an order book printed, and went all over Kansas taking orders for Osier willows, which they warranted to grow so high in two years they would make fences for the farms that no animals or blizzards could get over or through, and make shade for the houses and the whole farm. It was the year when the Osier willow craze was on and every farmer on the plains wanted to transform his prairie into a forest. Pa says the farmers fought with each other to sign orders, and some paid in advance, so as to get the willow cuttings in a hurry. Well, pa and the railroad man canvassed Kansas, and sold more than forty thousand millions of Osier willow cuttings, and put in the whole winter. In the spring, when it was time to deliver the goods, they went into the river bottoms and cut a whole lot of "pussy willow" cuttings, delivered them to the farmers and got their money, and went away. When the pussy willow cuttings died in their tracks, or grew up just plain pussy willows that never got high enough to hide a jack rabbit, the farmers of Kansas loaded their guns and waited for pa and the brakeman to come back to Kansas, but they never went back.

The brakeman became president of a great railroad, but when he has to go across the continent in his special car, he dodges Kansas, and goes across by the northern or southern route. Pa has so far dodged the farmers, but money wouldn't have hired him to stay with the circus and meet those farmers that they sold the willow gold bricks to. And yet, when I bunco anybody around the show, pa takes me one side and tells me that honesty is the best policy, and to never lie, 'cause my character as a man will depend on the start I make as a boy. He don't want me to go through life regretting the past, and being afraid of the cars for fear some act of my younger days will become known and queer me. I guess pa knows how it is hisself.

Well, if there is one thing I am proud of, it is that I have always been good. When I grow up to be a man, prosperous in business, and belonging to a church, and married, and have children growing up around me, I can put on an innocent face and a bold front, and point to my past with pride, if I should go to live among strangers, where nobody took the papers, and the people were not on to me. Pa says as long as your conscience is clear, and your pores open, life is one glad, sweet song. Well, I don't know, but if pa's conscience is clear, he must have strained it the way they do rain water, to get the wigglers out, or else he has used an egg to settle his conscience, the way they settle coffee. If his pores are open, he has opened them in the old way, with a corkscrew. But, with all I have had to contend with in the way of a frightful example from pa, I am not so worse.

How many boys of my age, do you suppose, could put in a season with a circus and have all the facilities I have had to go wrong, and come out as well as I have? The way the freaks just doted on me would have turned the heads of most boys, but when I found out that all of them, from the fat woman and the bearded woman, to the trapeze performers, ate onions three times a day, I said: "Nay, nay, Hennery will camp with the animals, whose smell is natural, and not acquired."

Say, do you know I have saved hundred of boys this summer from ruin, 'cause in every town there are lots of boys who want to run away from home and go off with a circus, and 'cause I belonged to the show they all came to me, and pa appointed me to discourage the boys, and drive them away from the show. I know in Virginia all the boys wanted to run away, and but for me the state wouldn't have boys enough to grow up and shoot the negroes. But when I found boys who wanted to skip away from home, I would give them a job, and they would have slept in the straw with the horses, and eaten at the second table after the negroes had been fed, if they could only shake their comfortable homes and loving friends and join a traveling circus.

Well, I always gave such boys a job watering the camels, and after they had carried water from daylight till dark, and had seen it disappear down a camel, and the camels grumbling because they didn't bring water faster, the boys would ask me how long it look to fill up a camel, anyway. I would tell them that if they kept right at work, the camels ought to be filled up full along in the fall. The boys would reluctantly resign. Our camels have been the making of hundreds of boys by their tank-like capacity to hold water. One boy at Richmond, Va., got it on me by getting a section of fire hose and hitching it to a hydrant, and letting the water run into a trough at the camel stand in the menagerie, and before I knew it the camels had filled up until they were swelled four times as big as they ought to be. Then they laid down, and couldn't march in the grand entree, and pa sent for a plumber to have the camels fixed with faucets. That boy was a genius, and we kept him and put him into the lemonade privilege. You can fill a camel with a hydrant all right, but if you bring the water in pails he will beat the game.

I remember one boy at Wilmington, Del., who insisted on going along with the show, 'cause his mother made him work after school, and my heart was touched, 'cause I know how a boy hates to work after school, so I gave him a job sprinkling insect powder on the buffaloes, that were scratching themselves against the tent poles so much that I felt they had something alive concealed about their persons. That boy started in with his can of insect powder on a buffalo calf, and then he filled the cow's hair full of the powder, and when he started on the bull, the bull took a sniff of the powder on the cow, and got it up his nose, and he held his head up kind of scared like, and turned his upper lip wrong-side out, and began to paw the ground. Then he made a charge on that boy, and tossed him through the tent, and I looked through the hole, and saw the boy scratching gravel towards town. If he is not running yet, he is probably doing chores for his mother both before and after school.

I have discouraged most of the boys who wanted to run away and go with the show, by giving them a curry comb and brush and telling them they could have a permanent job currying off the hyenas. Most boys would look sort of dubious about it, but would think it was up to them to be game, and they would take the curry comb and brush all right. I would take them to the cage, and tell them to just talk soothing to the hyenas through the bars, and when the hyenas began to get tame and act as though it would give them pleasure to be curried off, and laid down and rolled over, and purred like a cat that wanted to be scratched, and acted as though they would eat out of one's hand, the boys might call me, and I would have the cage opened and they could go in and curry them off.

Well, it would kill you dead to see a fool boy side up to a hyena cage and try to hypnotize a hyena by kind words and a pious example, saying soothing words like: "Soo, boss," or "O, come off now, and be a good fellow," and see the hyena snarl and show his teeth like an anarchist that a multi-millionaire might try to tame so he would take a roll of money out of his hand without biting the hand. I have had boys stand in front of a hyena cage with a curry-comb and brush all day, trying to get on good terms with the hyenas, and occasionally the hyenas would forget to snarl and the boy would think the animals were beginning to weaken, and the boy would work up closer to the cage, and say: "Pretty pussy," and hold out his hand and say: "Good fellow." Then the whole cageful of hyenas would make a rush for him, howling, snapping and scratching, with their bristles up, and the boy would fall backwards over a sacred cow. About this time I would come along and ask the boy if he had got the hyenas curried, 'cause if he had, I wanted him to curry the grave robbers--the jackals. Then the boy would reluctantly give up his tools, and say if I wanted the hyenas and jackals curried off I could do it myself. I would tell them they would never do for the circus business, 'cause faint heart never won fair hyena. Then they would go home and sell their mother's copper boiler to get money to pay their way in the show. Gee, but I have saved lots of boys from a circus fate.

Pa has an awful time in the hospital, 'cause twice a day the doctors strip him and pull a mess of cactus thorns out of him, and he yells and don't talk very pious. The doctor told me I must try and think of something to divert pa's mind from his suffering.

So I got some telegraph blanks and envelopes, and I have written messages from the show managers, twice a day. The morning message would tell about the business of the day before, and how they missed pa. Then I would add something like this: "The farmers around Olathe are all inquiring for you," or "The farmers around Topeka wish you were here, 'cause they want to give you a reception," or "About 200 farmers at Parsons think we ought to let them in free, on account of being old friends of yours." The last one broke pa all up. The message said: "Many farmers from Atchison are going to come with us to Kansas City to confer with you on an old matter of business." Pa jumped like a box car off the track, and wanted the doctors to send him to a hospital at St. Louis, and he told the doctors the reason, but they cheered him up by saying that if any mob came to the hospital after him, they would hide him in the pickling vat, and make the mob believe he was dead. That is the way it stands now. But pa is not so darn happy as I have seen him, though I try to do all I can to keep his mind off his trouble. I tell him as long as his conscience is clear, he is all right, but he says: "But, Hennery, that's the trouble; it ain't clear. Well, let us have peace, at any price."

CHAPTER XXV.

Pa Breaks in the Zebras and Drives a Six-in-Hand Team in the
Parade--The Freaks Have a Narrow Escape from Drowning.

Pa is stuck on the zebras. I do not know what there is about a zebra unless it is the wail paper effects of his exterior decoration that should make a man leave all the other animals and cleave unto the zebra, but pa has been putting in his leisure time all summer breaking the zebras to harness, and driving them single and double in the ring Sundays.

Everybody about the show knew pa was going to spring some surprise on us. I have tried to reason pa out of his unnatural infatuation for zebras, but you might as well talk to a rich old man who gets stuck on a chorus girl, and gives her all his money, and has to go and live at the poor house.

A zebra always looks to me like a joke that nature has played. Who, but nature, would ever think of laying out a plan for a zebra, and painting it in stripes, like a barber's pole, and yet we must admit that few human artists could paint a million zebras and get the stripes on as perfect as nature does with her eyes shut. The mule and the zebra are distant relatives, 'cause lots of mules have a few stripes on their legs, but the zebra is the eldest son who is aristocratic and inherits the stuff, while the mule is the younger son who never gets a look in for the money, but has to work for a living. So it is no wonder to me that the mule kicks. The zebra is the dude of the family, and the mule looks up to him, when he ought to kick his slats in, and rub out his stripes with a mule shoe eraser.

While pa was in the hospital at Kansas City he formed a plan to paralyze the town by driving six zebras to a tally-ho coach, in the parade, and the reporters interviewed pa, and the papers were full of it, and the people were wild with excitement, and everybody wanted to see a six-in-hand zebra team, driven by Alkali Ike, one of the greatest western stage drivers that was ever held up by road agents. Pa was to be Alkali Ike. The show struck Kansas City Sunday morning, and the management was scared at what pa had advertised to do, and they all wanted to call off the zebra stunt, but pa said if they cut it out the people would mob the show, so all day Sunday we hooked up the six zebras, and the hands led them around the tent with a mule with a bell on ridden in the lead. They seemed to go pretty well, but I could see pa's finish when he got out on the streets with that crazy team. Pa wanted all the freaks to ride on the tally-ho, and he had invited nine newspaper fellows to ride with him. Pa thought the zebra team would follow the bell mule ahead, like a 20-mule borax team would.

Well, Monday morning the parade started, and along about the middle of the parade, just ahead of the calliope, was pa and his six zebra team, his freaks and reporters, and pa handled the ribbons like a pirate. The fat woman sat on the driver's seat with pa, for ballast, and the rest of the freaks were sandwiched in between the reporters. We went along all right for half a mile, the circus hands walking beside the zebras, to kill them if they tried to jump over a house, while I rode the bell mule. If I had been planning the zebra business, I would have picked out a level town to try it on, but Kansas City is all hills and ravines, and going up hill the zebras' tally-ho had to be pushed by a couple of elephants, 'cause the zebras wouldn't pull the load, and going down hill we had to lock the wheels, and slide down.

When we got on the main street, where the crowd filled both sides, almost up to the team, and the people began to cheer, the zebras began to waltz and kick, and try to jump over each other, but the hands got them untangled, and we worried along, though pa was pale, and looked like a man smoking a cigar while sitting on an open powder keg. The fat woman grabbed pa every little while, and screamed that she wanted to get off and walk, but pa told her to hush up and try to be a man.

Well, as we were going down hill, by a park, near the Midland hotel, that confounded calliope had got right up behind the tally-ho, and the organist cut her loose, with the tune: "A Life on the Ocean Wave." Every zebra jumped into the air, the brake footpiece escaped pa's foot, and the tally-ho run on to the heels of the wheel zebras, and it was all off. There never was such a runaway since the days of Ben Hur. Pa had presence of mind enough to make the fat lady get down off the seat, and he put his feet on her to hold her down, the crowd yelled, and our zebras run into the cage ahead, containing the behemoth of Holy Writ, and knocked off a hind wheel, and every wagon ahead was either tipped over or disabled. The people fairly went wild, thinking the runaway was a part of the show. The giant fainted from fright, 'cause he always was a coward; the bearded woman threw her arms around a reporter, and scratched his face with her whiskers, while the Circassian girl got her white wig caught In the branch of a tree and lost it, and she was as bald as an ostrich egg. Pa took out the whip and larruped the zebras, to put some new stripes on them.

When we passed the camels they thought they were in the race, and they buckled in to keep up, and the chariot horses got the best of the drivers and they joined in. My mule kept up all right, and we went down the hill on to the level ground that runs to the Missouri river. When we got to the river the zebras turned short and tipped the tally-ho over into the water and the whole bunch on the coach was floundering in the muddy water; but there happened to be a sandbar under the water, so nobody was drowned, though we had to bail out the fat woman, she swallowed so much of the muddy river. The giant was senseless and two reporters got astride of him, thinking it was a rail, and drifted ashore, while pa laid on his back and floated like a duck, and when we got him out we found he had a life-preserver under his coat, and he said he put it on because he had a hunch that those zebras would make for running water if they ever got beyond control. Well, the crowd followed down to the river, and everybody was rescued, and the rest of the parade went over the route, and in the afternoon the tent was so full there were thousands standing up.

When pa came into the main tent with the zebras, in the grand parade around the ring, the crowd gave him three cheers, which probably caused the management to refrain from discharging him on the spot. Pa is like a cat, 'cause he always falls on his feet all right and he thinks the zebra tally-ho in the parade was the feature that caused the crowd to visit the show; but he says he will never drive zebras again, on account of the excitement.

The fat woman talks of having pa arrested for breaking one of her ribs when he held her down with his feet; but pa says his feet did not sink into her more than a foot or so, and he couldn't have hit a rib, nohow.

Well, I'm glad to be back in the show, 'cause there is more going on than there was in the hospital, where I put in a week while the doctors were pulling the cactus pin feathers out of pa that grew out on him in Indian Territory. Gee, but if I had to leave the circus business and go back to school, I know I should die of lonesomeness.

I got a chance to talk with pa at supper, and asked him if he was really crazy, as the hands say he is, and how he liked zebras, anyway, and he said: "Hennery, zebras are just people, they stampede just like politicians and bankers, and business men generally, and never know enough to let well enough alone. The mule is the only draft animal that always pulls straight and gets there right side up."

If I was going to run a circus for easy money, and a picnic, I wouldn't have any menagerie connected with it, 'cause the animals make more trouble than all the rest of the show. They are just like a lot of children in a reform school, they don't want to work, and they are just looking for a chance to fight when your back is turned, or to escape. They don't know where they would go if they did escape, but they don't want anybody over them, to teach them morals, though when meal time comes the reform school boys and the menagerie animals eat like tramps, because the food is so good, and then kick because it isn't better. If your performers in the circus proper do not suit you can discharge them, and if they are sick you can leave them in a hospital, and go on with the show, and forget about them until they show up in a week or two, pale as ghosts, and weak as cats, and demand back salary; but your animal has to be taken along and petted, and when you give him medicine to save his life, he will try to bite your hand off.

And yet you can't help getting stuck on the animals, and a man gets stuck on the kind of animal that is most like him. The grizzly old granger, who never buttons the collar of his shirt, and whose Adam's apple looks like a hen's head, will stay by the camels, hours at a time, the pious church man feels at home among the sacred cattle, the strong-arm holdup man will linger by the grizzly bear, the prize-fighter will haunt the lions' den, the garroter will gaze lovingly at the tigers, the sneak thief seems to love the hyenas, and the big game hunters watch the deer and elk. Some of us who have brains love the monkeys, they are so human.

CHAPTER XXVI.

The Rings Are So Muddy the Performers Have to Wear Rubber Boots--The
Freaks Present Pa with a Big Heart of Roses--The Show Closes and the
Bad Boy Starts West with His Pa in Search of Attractions for the
Coming Season.

Well, Missouri is the state to teach a circus humility, and we have taken the thirty-third degree in the last ten days. It has rained nine days and a half out of a possible ten days, and the mud is something we never dreamed of before. The wagons have been mired in the mud on the way from the train to the lot every day in the streets of cities big enough to have street cars and electric lights. The cities have one or two main streets paved, but the rest of the streets are just virgin soil, and you have got to swim to get to the paved streets. When you start away for the lot, it is like Washington crossing the Delaware.

And yet the people come from miles around to see the show, and everybody rides a web-footed mule, that can wallow in the mud. They hitch the mules to fences outside the tent, and while the performance is going on the mules bray in concert and drown the band.

Pa has been wild ever since we struck Missouri, and no wonder, 'cause everybody seems to lay everything in the way of weather on him. Every place we show the lot is one sea of mud, and when we get the rings made they seem like a chain of lakes, and in galloping around the rings the horses splash mud and water clear to the reserved seats. The riders of the horses have to come out in rubber hunting boots and when they get on the horses we have to pull their boots off and hold them until the act is over, then the riders sit on the horses and pull the boots on and get down in the mud of the ring and bow to the audience.

The woman riders are the worst to wear rubber boots, 'cause they fall down in the mud and spoil their dresses and kick scandalous, The trapeze performers have to be carried out of the dressing room on stretchers, and hoisted up to the net, 'cause they can't do stunts up on the trapeze with wet feet, and we have worked ourselves to death getting things in shape.

The confounded elephants just glory in the mud, and the minute they get in the ring they all lay down and roll in the mud and water, so when they are ready to do their act they look like walking mud pies. The freaks are awful to handle, the giant being the only one that can wade through and look pleasant, and the fat woman would make you weary, she has to be carried back and forth to the platform by half a force of hands. Pa has had shawl straps and coffin handles fastened to her clothes, so there will be something to grab hold of to move her around. I don't think that another year we will have any fat woman, 'cause pa says it costs more to get this 500-pound female from one place to another than all the rest of the show. He thinks that people who visit the show don't care much about a fat woman anyway, but just guy her and ask her what kind of breakfast food she lives on. He thinks if we had three reasonably fat women that weighed about 200 pounds apiece, it would give better satisfaction and they would be easier to handle; but when she heard what pa said and felt that she was going to be shook next year she began to cry, and it was like turning on water in a bathtub. Pa had to pet her and then the bearded woman got jealous.

At Jefferson City there came a cold wave and everything was froze stiff, and you could skate in the rings, and the management decided to get to St. Louis and send the show to winter quarters, and organize for next season. So we have had a time closing up for the season, and sending the animals to the barns on our farm up north, and discharging and paying off the performers and bidding everybody goodby. We have bought presents for everybody, and it has been a picnic.

Pa had a big heart, with roses all around it, made of a horse collar, covered with flowers, which came from the freaks, and the performers remembered him with presents, and pa gave everybody something, and everybody got together in the main tent and made speeches.

The manager thanked everybody and promised that next year we would have the greatest show on earth. He said the management had decided that what we lacked this year was a wild west show, as the people everywhere seemed to dote on busting broncos, and roping cattle, and chasing buffaloes and seeing Indians and rough riders chase up and down the arena. He felt that in justice to our rough-riding president, it was proper to have a wild west show that would make things hum next year. He said he took pleasure in informing the people of the show that pa had been commissioned to go out west at once and secure the Indians and cowboys, horses that buck and bounce off the riders, cattle that would stand it to be lassoed and thrown down for the amusement of the public, buffaloes that would bellow and act like old times on the plains, stage coaches and robbers, and he promised that next year they would have no cause to be ashamed of the show. He said pa was authorized to spare no expense to round up a wild west show second to none. The performers and hands cheered the manager, and then they yelled for pa for a speech.

Pa got up on the tub that the elephants stand on, and said that it was true what the manager said about a wild west show, and that he was proud of the confidence reposed in him. He should be glad to take an expedition and go out into the far west and beard the wild west Indian in his tepee and engage Indians by the hundred to come with us next year. He would pierce the wilderness of the west in search of the wildest red men and would hunt the cowboy in his lair and secure those who could make the most trouble for cattle and horses and shoot up an audience if necessary to keep the peace, and he would buy buffaloes enough so every performer could ride one if he wanted to. He said while we had this year had some attempts at a wild west department in our show, it was only a tame imitation of what we would have next year, and he wanted them all to pray for him, that he might come out of the wild far west without being killed. He said he should take Hennery along with him as a mascot, and if the worst came he could trade me to an Indian tribe for ponies, or leave me as a hostage with some tribe until he returned the Indians at the close of next season. Pa closed his remarks by hoping that nothing had occurred during the past season that would cause anybody to have it in for him, 'cause he had tried to be impartial in his cussedness, and while he felt that he had been considered an interloper in the profession at first, he had found that everybody looked upon him later in the season as the main guy in the show, and that all had felt at liberty to give it to him in the neck on every proper occasion and he felt that he had taken his medicine like a thoroughbred.

They gave three cheers for pa, and then they brought in the blankets and tossed everybody up until they lost everything out of their pockets and yelled that they had enough, and they wound up by tossing pa up in the blanket until he could see stars. They were going to give the fat woman a hoist, when the boss canvasman gave the signal to take down the tents, and all was in a hubbub for about 15 minutes.

When everything was down and everybody went to the train, after joining hands around the middle ring and singing "Old Lang Sine," pa and I and the managers went to a hotel to organize our expedition to the far west in search of talent for a wild west show that shall be the greatest ever put under canvas. After all had gone away, and only pa and I and the managers were left, it seemed, as we thought over the incidents of the past season, as though there had been an earthquake and the whole show had been blotted out of existence.

Pa choked up and was going to cry, and I got my throat full of something so I could not speak, and the managers began to wipe their eyes, and pa saved the day by saying: "Oh, what's the use, let's order up some highballs," and when they came, with a red lemonade for me, pa said: "Well, here's to the people that crowd around the ticket wagon and fight to get the first ticket when the window is open, and go away after the show and say it is the greatest show ever."

"Hey Rube!" said the manager, and we drank standing, and pa went out and bought tickets for Cheyenne, and some beads, to give to the Indians we shall visit in the west.

www.bookjungle.com *email: sales@bookjungle.com fax: 630-214-0564 mail: Book Jungle PO Box 2226 Champaign, IL 61825*

The Codes Of Hammurabi And Moses
W. W. Davies

QTY

The discovery of the Hammurabi Code is one of the greatest achievements of archaeology, and is of paramount interest, not only to the student of the Bible, but also to all those interested in ancient history...

Religion   **ISBN:** *1-59462-338-4*   **Pages:132**
MSRP $12.95

The Theory of Moral Sentiments
Adam Smith

QTY

This work from 1749. contains original theories of conscience amd moral judgment and it is the foundation for systemof morals.

Philosophy   ISBN: *1-59462-777-0*   **Pages:536**
MSRP $19.95

Jessica's First Prayer
Hesba Stretton

QTY

In a screened and secluded corner of one of the many railway-bridges which span the streets of London there could be seen a few years ago, from five o'clock every morning until half past eight, a tidily set-out coffee-stall, consisting of a trestle and board, upon which stood two large tin cans, with a small fire of charcoal burning under each so as to keep the coffee boiling during the early hours of the morning when the work-people were thronging into the city on their way to their daily toil...

Pages:84

Childrens   ISBN: *1-59462-373-2*   *MSRP $9.95*

My Life and Work
Henry Ford

QTY

Henry Ford revolutionized the world with his implementation of mass production for the Model T automobile. Gain valuable business insight into his life and work with his own auto-biography... "We have only started on our development of our country we have not as yet, with all our talk of wonderful progress, done more than scratch the surface. The progress has been wonderful enough but..."

Pages:300

Biographies/   ISBN: *1-59462-198-5*   *MSRP $21.95*

The Art of Cross-Examination
Francis Wellman

QTY

I presume it is the experience of every author, after his first book is published upon an important subject, to be almost overwhelmed with a wealth of ideas and illustrations which could readily have been included in his book, and which to his own mind, at least, seem to make a second edition inevitable. Such certainly was the case with me; and when the first edition had reached its sixth impression in five months, I rejoiced to learn that it seemed to my publishers that the book had met with a sufficiently favorable reception to justify a second and considerably enlarged edition. ...

Pages:412

Reference   **ISBN: *1-59462-647-2*** *MSRP $19.95*

On the Duty of Civil Disobedience
Henry David Thoreau

QTY

Thoreau wrote his famous essay, On the Duty of Civil Disobedience, as a protest against an unjust but popular war and the immoral but popular institution of slave-owning. He did more than write—he declined to pay his taxes, and was hauled off to gaol in consequence. Who can say how much this refusal of his hastened the end of the war and of slavery ?

Law   **ISBN: *1-59462-747-9***

Pages:48

MSRP $7.45

Dream Psychology Psychoanalysis for Beginners
Sigmund Freud

QTY

Sigmund Freud, born Sigismund Schlomo Freud (May 6, 1856 - September 23, 1939), was a Jewish-Austrian neurologist and psychiatrist who co-founded the psychoanalytic school of psychology. Freud is best known for his theories of the unconscious mind, especially involving the mechanism of repression; his redefinition of sexual desire as mobile and directed towards a wide variety of objects; and his therapeutic techniques, especially his understanding of transference in the therapeutic relationship and the presumed value of dreams as sources of insight into unconscious desires.

Pages:196

Psychology   **ISBN: *1-59462-905-6*** *MSRP $15.45*

The Miracle of Right Thought
Orison Swett Marden

QTY

Believe with all of your heart that you will do what you were made to do. When the mind has once formed the habit of holding cheerful, happy, prosperous pictures, it will not be easy to form the opposite habit. It does not matter how improbable or how far away this realization may see, or how dark the prospects may be, if we visualize them as best we can, as vividly as possible, hold tenaciously to them and vigorously struggle to attain them, they will gradually become actualized, realized in the life. But a desire, a longing without endeavor, a yearning abandoned or held indifferently will vanish without realization.

Pages:360

Self Help   **ISBN: *1-59462-644-8*** *MSRP $25.45*

The Rosicrucian Cosmo-Conception Mystic Christianity *by Max Heindel*   ISBN: *1-59462-188-8*   **$38.95**
The Rosicrucian Cosmo-conception is not dogmatic, neither does it appeal to any other authority than the reason of the student. It is: not controversial, but is: sent forth in the, hope that it may help to clear...   New Age/Religion Pages 646

Abandonment To Divine Providence *by Jean-Pierre de Caussade*   ISBN: *1-59462-228-0*   **$25.95**
"The Rev. Jean Pierre de Caussade was one of the most remarkable spiritual writers of the Society of Jesus in France in the 18th Century. His death took place at Toulouse in 1751. His works have gone through many editions and have been republished...   Inspirational/Religion Pages 400

Mental Chemistry *by Charles Haanel*   ISBN: *1-59462-192-6*   **$23.95**
Mental Chemistry allows the change of material conditions by combining and appropriately utilizing the power of the mind. Much like applied chemistry creates something new and unique out of careful combinations of chemicals the mastery of mental chemistry...   New Age Pages 354

The Letters of Robert Browning and Elizabeth Barret Barrett 1845-1846 vol II   ISBN: *1-59462-193-4*   **$35.95**
by Robert Browning and Elizabeth Barrett   Biographies Pages 596

Gleanings In Genesis (volume I) *by Arthur W. Pink*   ISBN: *1-59462-130-6*   **$27.45**
Appropriately has Genesis been termed "the seed plot of the Bible" for in it we have, in germ form, almost all of the great doctrines which are afterwards fully developed in the books of Scripture which follow...   Religion/Inspirational Pages 420

The Master Key *by L. W. de Laurence*   ISBN: *1-59462-001-6*   **$30.95**
In no branch of human knowledge has there been a more lively increase of the spirit of research during the past few years than in the study of Psychology, Concentration and Mental Discipline. The requests for authentic lessons in Thought Control, Mental Discipline and...   New Age/Business Pages 422

The Lesser Key Of Solomon Goetia *by L. W. de Laurence*   ISBN: *1-59462-092-X*   **$9.95**
This translation of the first book of the "Lernegton" which is now for the first time made accessible to students of Talismanic Magic was done, after careful collation and edition, from numerous Ancient Manuscripts in Hebrew, Latin, and French...   New Age/Occult Pages 92

Rubaiyat Of Omar Khayyam *by Edward Fitzgerald*   ISBN: *1-59462-332-5*   **$13.95**
Edward Fitzgerald, whom the world has already learned, in spite of his own efforts to remain within the shadow of anonymity, to look upon as one of the rarest poets of the century, was born at Bredfield, in Suffolk, on the 31st of March, 1809. He was the third son of John Purcell...   Music Pages 172

Ancient Law *by Henry Maine*   ISBN: *1-59462-128-4*   **$29.95**
The chief object of the following pages is to indicate some of the earliest ideas of mankind, as they are reflected in Ancient Law, and to point out the relation of those ideas to modern thought.   Religiom/History Pages 452

Far-Away Stories *by William J. Locke*   ISBN: *1-59462-129-2*   **$19.45**
"Good wine needs no bush, but a collection of mixed vintages does. And this book is just such a collection. Some of the stories I do not want to remain buried for ever in the museum files of dead magazine-numbers an author's not unpardonable vanity..."   Fiction Pages 272

Life of David Crockett *by David Crockett*   ISBN: *1-59462-250-7*   **$27.45**
"Colonel David Crockett was one of the most remarkable men of the times in which he lived. Born in humble life, but gifted with a strong will, an indomitable courage, and unremitting perseverance...   Biographies/New Age Pages 424

Lip-Reading *by Edward Nitchie*   ISBN: *1-59462-206-X*   **$25.95**
Edward B. Nitchie, founder of the New York School for the Hard of Hearing, now the Nitchie School of Lip-Reading, Inc, wrote "LIP-READING Principles and Practice". The development and perfecting of this meritorious work on lip-reading was an undertaking...   How-to Pages 400

A Handbook of Suggestive Therapeutics, Applied Hypnotism, Psychic Science   ISBN: *1-59462-214-0*   **$24.95**
by Henry Munro   Health/New Age/Health/Self-help Pages 376

A Doll's House: and Two Other Plays *by Henrik Ibsen*   ISBN: *1-59462-112-8*   **$19.95**
Henrik Ibsen created this classic when in revolutionary 1848 Rome. Introducing some striking concepts in playwriting for the realist genre, this play has been studied the world over.   Fiction/Classics/Plays 308

The Light of Asia *by sir Edwin Arnold*   ISBN: *1-59462-204-3*   **$13.95**
In this poetic masterpiece, Edwin Arnold describes the life and teachings of Buddha. The man who was to become known as Buddha to the world was born as Prince Gautama of India but he rejected the worldly riches and abandoned the reigns of power when...   Religion/History/Biographies Pages 170

The Complete Works of Guy de Maupassant *by Guy de Maupassant*   ISBN: *1-59462-157-8*   **$16.95**
"For days and days, nights and nights, I had dreamed of that first kiss which was to consecrate our engagement, and I knew not on what spot I should put my lips..."   Fiction/Classics Pages 240

The Art of Cross-Examination *by Francis L. Wellman*   ISBN: *1-59462-309-0*   **$26.95**
Written by a renowned trial lawyer, Wellman imparts his experience and uses case studies to explain how to use psychology to extract desired information through questioning.   How-to/Science/Reference Pages 408

Answered or Unanswered? *by Louisa Vaughan*   ISBN: *1-59462-248-5*   **$10.95**
Miracles of Faith in China   Religion Pages 112

The Edinburgh Lectures on Mental Science (1909) *by Thomas*   ISBN: *1-59462-008-3*   **$11.95**
This book contains the substance of a course of lectures recently given by the writer in the Queen Street Hall, Edinburgh. Its purpose is to indicate the Natural Principles governing the relation between Mental Action and Material Conditions...   New Age/Psychology Pages 148

Ayesha *by H. Rider Haggard*   ISBN: *1-59462-301-5*   **$24.95**
Verily and indeed it is the unexpected that happens! Probably if there was one person upon the earth from whom the Editor of this, and of a certain previous history, did not expect to hear again...   Classics Pages 380

Ayala's Angel *by Anthony Trollope*   ISBN: *1-59462-352-X*   **$29.95**
The two girls were both pretty, but Lucy who was twenty-one who supposed to be simple and comparatively unattractive, whereas Ayala was credited, as her Bombwhat romantic name might show, with poetic charm and a taste for romance. Ayala when her father died was nineteen...   Fiction Pages 484

The American Commonwealth *by James Bryce*   ISBN: *1-59462-286-8*   **$34.45**
An interpretation of American democratic political theory. It examines political mechanics and society from the perspective of Scotsman James Bryce   Politics Pages 572

Stories of the Pilgrims *by Margaret P. Pumphrey*   ISBN: *1-59462-116-0*   **$17.95**
This book explores pilgrims religious oppression in England as well as their escape to Holland and eventual crossing to America on the Mayflower, and their early days in New England...   History Pages 268

www.bookjungle.com *email: sales@bookjungle.com fax: 630-214-0564 mail: Book Jungle PO Box 2226 Champaign, IL 61825*

QTY

The Fasting Cure *by Sinclair Upton* ISBN: *1-59462-222-1* **$13.95**

In the Cosmopolitan Magazine for May, 1910, and in the Contemporary Review (London) for April, 1910, I published an article dealing with my experiences in fasting. I have written a great many magazine articles, but never one which attracted so much attention... New Age/Self Help/Health Pages 164

Hebrew Astrology *by Sepharial* ISBN: *1-59462-308-2* **$13.45**

In these days of advanced thinking it is a matter of common observation that we have left many of the old landmarks behind and that we are now pressing forward to greater heights and to a wider horizon than that which represented the mind-content of our progenitors... Astrology Pages 144

Thought Vibration or The Law of Attraction in the Thought World ISBN: *1-59462-127-6* **$12.95**

by William Walker Atkinson *Psychology/Religion Pages 144*

Optimism *by Helen Keller* ISBN: *1-59462-108-X* **$15.95**

Helen Keller was blind, deaf, and mute since 19 months old, yet famously learned how to overcome these handicaps, and spread her lectures promoting optimism. An inspiring read for everyone... Biographies/Inspirational Pages 84

Sara Crewe *by Frances Burnett* ISBN: *1-59462-360-0* **$9.45**

In the first place, Miss Minchin lived in London. Her home was a large, dull, tall one, in a large, dull square, where all the houses were alike, and all the sparrows were alike, and where all the door-knockers made the same heavy sound... Childrens/Classic Pages 88

The Autobiography of Benjamin Franklin *by Benjamin Franklin* ISBN: *1-59462-135-7* **$24.95**

The Autobiography of Benjamin Franklin has probably been more extensively read than any other American historical work, and no other book of its kind has had such ups and downs of fortune. Franklin lived for many years in England, where he was agent... Biographies/History Pages 332

Name	
Email	
Telephone	
Address	
City, State ZIP	

☐ **Credit Card**   ☐ **Check / Money Order**

Credit Card Number	
Expiration Date	
Signature	

Please Mail to: Book Jungle
PO Box 2226
Champaign, IL 61825
or Fax to: 630-214-0564

ORDERING INFORMATION

web: *www.bookjungle.com*
email: *sales@bookjungle.com*
fax: *630-214-0564*
mail: *Book Jungle PO Box 2226 Champaign, IL 61825*
or PayPal *to sales@bookjungle.com*

Please contact us for bulk discounts

DIRECT-ORDER TERMS

**20% Discount if You Order
Two or More Books**
Free Domestic Shipping!
Accepted: Master Card, Visa,
Discover, American Express